"My dear Lady Kathryn, will you do me the great honor of becoming my wife?"

Kat was numb with horror, had been since her entire family burst through the door, and she discovered herself in bed with a stranger. But his calm acceptance of Lady Tutwilliger's outrageous suggestion restored her natural spirit.

"My lord, that's a terrible idea! We are total strangers!" she argued.

"Lady Kathryn, in the ton, more often than not, strangers readily become betrothed," he answered quietly. . . .

"This entire incident is totally, utterly ridiculous! You and I know nothing untoward happened between us. We must simply make the rest of them all see reason."

Also by Leslie Lynn
Published by Fawcett Books:

RAKE'S REDEMPTION

SCANDAL'S CHILD

Leslie Lynn

FAWCETT CREST • NEW YORK

With love to our children—
Heidi, Alan, Jeff, Michael,
Lauren, Kathryn, David, Rod,
Karen, and Olivia

A Fawcett Crest Book
Published by Ballantine Books
Copyright © 1990 by Elaine Sima and Sherrill Bodine

Library of Congress Catalog Card Number: 90-93131

ISBN 0-449-21931-3

Manufactured in the United States of America

First Edition: October 1990

Prologue

Early morning mist shrouded the crenelated towers that gave the Crawford family seat its name—Culter Towers. Once the scene of so much unhappiness, the Towers had come to life again with the advent of the new mistress, Juliana, and the obvious contentment of its master, Dominic.

There was a joy here now that made Jules wish to linger with his half brother, but his task was completed. It was time to take his leave. He paced restlessly across the carriage drive, his black traveling cloak billowing behind him. At the far side he paused to peer one last time through the dim light at the hill that held the graves of his mother and stepfather.

Unlike his brother, Dominic, who was only half-French, Jules's utterly Gallic soul had long ago accepted the constant ache of regret. Now, to his surprise, for the first time in over ten years it was nearly gone. Perhaps, at last, the brothers could put their past behind them.

A robust wail pierced the quiet dawn and Jules turned to smile at Dominic's practiced attempts to quiet Lord Giles Robert Alexander Crawford, aged six weeks.

"I told you not to wake the babe, Dominic," Jules

scolded, reaching out to stroke his nephew's tiny fist. Giles's miniature fingers immediately clasped Jules's finger and tried to carry it to his rosebud baby mouth.

Gently extricating himself, while at the same time encouraging his nephew to drool on his own thumb, Jules's gaze met his brother's cornflower blue eyes, and they both burst into laughter.

How good it was to share this moment!

Jules's relief that Dominic had finally escaped the dark memories of the past was tinged with sadness at his parting. The love and contentment he had watched develop and grow between Dominic and Juliana had extended to include him in their small family. They had even asked him to stand godfather to their precious son. But now he had to leave.

"I know you planned to travel light and fast to the coast, Jules. Good of you to indulge Juliana and deliver the gift."

"*Mon frère,* she has just made me an uncle. Her every whim is as much my delight to fulfill as it is yours." Jules shrugged. "Besides it is little enough to make a stop at this Blue Boar Inn. And I confess a certain curiosity about Mrs. Forbes. Juliana has painted a most interesting picture."

Jiggling the baby carefully in his arms, Dominic smiled. "Juliana insists Mrs. Forbes is a gypsy princess who read her palm and saw our future together. She's convinced Mrs. Forbes has the *eye* or some such thing. But, she didn't have to be a fortune-teller to see I was smitten nearly at the first sight of Juliana."

Recalling Dominic's long, and once unsavory, reputation where women were concerned, Jules became even more intrigued with the proprietor of the Blue Boar Inn.

"I shall deliver the good tidings of young Lord Crawford." Unable to resist a last touch, Jules ran the side of one finger over Giles's soft rosy cheek, but the baby was fast asleep and did not stir.

Jules had delayed long enough. Now that Dominic was happily settled, it was time he began to sort out his own life.

"I hate farewells, *mon frère*," he said brusquely, stepping back.

Dominic's clear gaze rested solemnly upon him. "Culter Towers will always be your home. Do not stay from us too long this time."

Their parting, so different than it had been years earlier, caused Jules to clasp his brother's shoulders fondly, careful not to jar the sleeping bundle.

"It is a promise."

Jules grasped the reins of his patiently waiting horse, Noir, and threw them over his head. The stallion blew softly and stamped, as if acknowledging that it was time to go. Without another word Jules mounted and cantered down the driveway. At the near gate he turned and waved, then disappeared into the low-hanging mist.

This parting was different, tinged with regret, not bitterness. Dominic's life was finally all it should be: surrounded by a loving wife and faithful friends, he could take his rightful place in the world. There was no such place for Jules Devereaux, Comte de Saville. France was his birth country, but, truly, after spending his formative years in England, he found it hard to return there.

Return he must, though! His own father's estate, confiscated during Napoleon's reign, had been returned to his keeping, and although his man of business had painted a dismal picture, it was his ancestral home. But he held only vague memories of it, having fled France with his mother as a small child.

Odd, during this twelve month sojourn in England he had not once thought of his life in the last ten years since the accident—the wandering from place to place, the women. His future lay before him. Perhaps this Mrs. Forbes could tell him what it held. He laughed at himself, aware of a strange eagerness to meet this innkeeper his enchanting sister-in-law held in such fondness, to see the place where his brother's life had begun anew.

Mrs. Forbes was the tiniest woman Jules had ever seen. Her face was as brown as a roasted nut and bore the marks of many years, yet her eyes were alert and piercingly direct. She accepted the news of Giles's birth and the miniature of Dominic, Juliana, and baby with a graciousness beyond her station.

"It's just as I saw it." Her thin face creased into a network of tiny lines as she nodded positively. "Now I'll show you to your room, Comte. It's the same one I gave your brother."

The chamber she took him to in the upper reaches of the inn was clean and neat—certainly better appointed than might be expected—just as the meal of roasted chicken with stewed mushrooms, lamb fries, roasted potatoes, tongue stewed with peppercorns, and a dish of fresh green peas, followed by butter cake with huge strawberries was unexceptionable.

All in all it was much as he had hoped, this inn

where his brother had finally found his wonderful Juliana. He had always loved his brother and now he also envied him. There was little doubt he would never find such contentment, for his scars from the past were so much more obvious.

Sipping his port, Jules sat back, and the buxom serving girl leaned over, letting her blouse gape open as she poured into his glass. This was the only mar on the evening, the obvious advances of this wench.

Jules was not vain. How could he be, he snorted with derision. A scarred cheek and a blind eye requiring a riband could hardly be considered handsome. But he had discovered over the years that his appearance seemed to fascinate some women. A certain type of woman—not the kind he could come to love, who would give him a home and, he thought of Giles, children.

He had never given much thought to the future before. He had lived day to day, but now, after the months spent at Culter Towers with Juliana and Dominic, he couldn't help but regret theirs was a life he would never have. His old ways seemed suddenly meaningless. How could any lady of quality be able to overlook his scars? If her romantic nature led her to think he had been maimed fighting Boney, she was due for a surprise.

There was nothing romantic about the truth, he thought grimly, tossing down the last of his port.

Refusing to dwell on that particular memory, he rose slowly to his feet and ascended the inn's narrow stairway, to the serving girl's pouting regret.

He was simply not in the mood for that kind of dalliance. His intention was for an early night, but to his surprise, Mrs. Forbes waited outside his chamber.

Smiling, he bowed. "My compliments on supper. It was superb."

She nodded as regally as some great lady of the ton. Something about the proud way she held herself prodded Jules to lift her fingers for a fleeting kiss. Shocked by his own actions, he didn't protest when she clasped his hand firmly and turned it over. He allowed the familiarity, somewhat amused by the idea of having his palm read.

But there was nothing humorous about the look on Mrs. Forbes's face. Her piercing eyes bore into him.

"You have had a long journey through many empty chambers. Now the wrong door will be the right one for you. Although you do not believe, the contentment you have seen can be yours."

Chapter 1

"THE TWO OF you shall be the death of me!" Lady Tutwilliger gasped, falling back upon the large pillows of her day bed. "Someone fetch the smelling salts!"

Lady Kathryn Thistlewait shared a speaking glance with her elder sister, Lady Mariah.

"Willy, you know you have never had the vapors in your entire life. Do stop being so missish," Kat declared firmly.

That sentiment caused her godmother to open her eyes, sit up straighter, and pin her with a steely stare. "You unfeeling child! It is only because I possess the constitution of my late father, Lord Frogmorton, that I can withstand your antics. How else would I have survived your crying off from Lord Barton and Mariah turning down the Duke of Bromston last Season."

Mariah tossed her dark springy curls. "The duke is old enough to be my father! He has a dreadful laugh, much like a baying hound, that always draws unwelcome attention. But worst of all, his cravats are always imperfectly tied."

"And I was much too fond of dear Lord Barton to marry him without love," Kat interjected quickly.

"You have long told us, dear Willy, that we must follow our hearts."

"Yes, we are, as always, only following your unexceptional example," Mariah added sweetly.

"You are both full of Banbury Tales, and we all know it," Lady Tutwilliger snorted. "But this nonsense must cease now, this very instant, or we will all be undone."

"But, Willy, the Season has only just began. We have been on our very best behavior," Mariah fretted, absently patting a coil of hair although it fell perfectly, as always, about her heart-shaped face.

"This Season is only one week old, so of course you have done nothing wrong. Except that Jacko did not make the dinner party for the Vanderworths. The boy is too vexing. Miss Helen Vanderworth's twenty-five thousand pounds a year is nothing to sneeze at, even if she is from the colonies."

"But, Willy, I find both Miss Vanderworth and her brother correct on all forms. In fact, Mr. Vanderworth often puts our own gentlemen to the blush."

Kat stared at her sister in surprise. Except for refusing the Duke of Bromston, Mariah had always been a pattern card of decorum. Kat had, in all truth, not paid much attention to Mr. Christian Vanderworth, but if Mariah praised him, his manners must be utterly flawless.

"Yes, he does possess a certain air about him that is pleasing. But it is *your* behavior that concerns me. Your willful actions last Season got the tattles talking again about the 'Thistlewait Jilting Scandal.'" Lady Tutwilliger's impressive bosom rose to alarming proportions. "Not that your dear late father didn't do exactly the correct thing to cry off from that dreadful Lady Annabelle Thurston and marry your sweet Mama, for Annabelle drove her husband to an early grave. But recalling the scandal did your expectations no good. However, *my* credit shall bring us all about. Just promise me you shall be perfect models of decorum this Season."

Her gaze fell upon Kat, for Mariah was usually perfection itself, both in behavior and dress.

Instantly Kat noticed the smudges at the hem of her saffron walking dress. Really, it wasn't fair! Mariah had walked on the same path in Hyde Park and there wasn't a mark on her peach skirt. Her guilty look merely called attention to her plight.

"Kat, you must try to be more careful of your things. I don't know how we'll go on if you are constantly getting smudged, or leaving your things where they don't belong. People will begin to think you're nothing but a ninnyhammer."

Kat could do naught but nod. She would just have to do better. Although she had always viewed her parent's elopement with a romantic eye and vowed to herself to find true love before she wed, she was equally devoted to Lady Tutwilliger and Mariah. She would do nothing more to upset dear Willy or further mar Mariah's chances to be happily settled.

"I promise, Willy. I shall be so good you'll find me positively boring," Kat declared with real feeling.

Lady Tutwilliger did not appear completely convinced, but she nodded. "Thank you, Kathryn. Now if I can just find your dreadful twin and exact a promise from him we shall be all right and tight. Hannah!"

Kat started. She had forgotten Lady Hannah Hamilton was in the room.

Yawning delicately, her hair as gray-brown as

her eyes and dress, the mousy woman rose slowly from the chair in front of the fireplace. A distant cousin of Willy's, Hannah Hamilton had been her constant companion for as long as Kat could remember. Supposedly a personal secretary, Hannah cosseted Lady Tutwilliger and pandered to her every whim. But if Willy had inherited her strong will from her late father, then Hannah had surely been no relation of his. For, at the first sign of conflict, Hannah always sought escape in a short nap.

"Hannah, pen a letter to Jacko and demand he attend me at once!" Lady Tutwilliger commanded before turning her attention back to the girls. "Be off with you, and dress for Lady Sefton's musicale. Everyone shall be in attendance, and I want you to look your very best. Tonight the Thistlewaits shall once again take on the ton!"

Kat's nerves were evidenced by restless pacing, back and forth from the Carrara marble fireplace to the green brocade draperies at the parlor windows that faced the street. Society itself didn't frighten her, not even the strict rules that sometimes chafed. Rules for curtseying, rules for walking, rules for smiling . . . Sometimes she even wished to be back in the country where all the rules had seemed a game. Sometimes . . . but not tonight.

Tonight was important for all of them. She wouldn't let Willy down again. Mariah had to make a match this Season, and Jacko . . . Drat! When would he make an appearance? His future was at stake here, too! It wasn't like him to desert them in their hour of need.

A noise in the hall stopped her in midstride; her fingers began to anxiously pleat the soft folds of

10

rose moire silk that fell from the empire waist of her evening dress. Jacko?

But no impetuous twin appeared.

Suddenly realizing Lady Tutwilliger would ring a fine peal over her should her gown be creased, Kat crossed back to the window to finger open the drapes and peer into the street.

"Kat, whatever are you doing?"

Mariah's scandalized tone brought her about abruptly. She dropped the curtain guiltily. "I thought I heard Jacko."

"I'm going to give him a piece of my mind when he finally graces us with his presence," Mariah fretted.

"I can understand why Jacko is not dancing attendance, Mariah. Willy has been playing matchmaker rather blatantly."

"Of course you would defend him!" Mariah scolded. "It is too vexing of him. What will the Vanderworths think?"

Mariah stepped in front of the rosewood mirror to tug gently at a periwinkle blue ribbon threaded through her glossy brown curls that fell in lustrous perfection about her heart-shaped face. The color exactly matched the overslip and was repeated in tiny bows edging the short puffy sleeves of her gown.

Both girls possessed the Thistlewait heavily lashed aquamarine eyes, but Mariah was diminutive and softly rounded, like their mother had been, whereas Kat was willowy, barely two inches shorter than Jacko, and blond like their father. However, all three had an abundance of the Thistlewait stubbornness, which made Kat more than ever fearful of Jacko's whereabouts.

"Kat, don't look so worried." Mariah suddenly

smiled, two charming dimples appearing on her rose-colored cheeks, and patted her sister's hand. "You mustn't appear pinched-faced at Lady Sefton's tonight. Jacko will turn up soon."

"Yes, the boy must appear soon!" Lady Tutwilliger boomed, sailing into the room, the lilac feather in her turban quivering. "I hope he will appear tonight, since he cried off from *my* dinner party for Miss Vanderworth and her brother. Whatever will they think?"

"The Vanderworths are so very pleasant, Willy, I'm sure they will understand," Mariah placated automatically, but her eyes flew questioningly to Kat's face.

Kat had never before seen that particular expression upon her sister's beautiful countenance. Yes, she really must be more attentive at these ton parties and take a good long look at the Vanderworths. She would have to stop worrying about Jacko and only hope he would do nothing to endanger this Season. It meant so much to Willy and Mariah. She had already vowed to be on her best behavior.

Jacko was not at Lady Sefton's musicale, although half the ton was in attendance. Squeezed into all the salons, drinking champagne and devouring lobster patties, the ton was more than prepared for the onset of the Season. Yet, only a week into the whirl of balls, parties, and routs Kat was already bored with being in the midst of yet another sad crush.

The press of people shifted around them and Mariah grabbed Kat's arm; with gentle pressure she indicated a direction. "There they are!" she whispered, hardly allowing herself a glance.

Kat had no such compunction. A tall, impeccably dressed gentleman, his cravat tied with painstaking neatness, strolled toward them. On his arm was a pale young woman, wearing a demurely cut white crepe gown. The girl's squint was quite pronounced until they drew closer, and then she smiled. Quite a pleasing feature in an otherwise unremarkable face, Kat thought, as Miss Helen Vanderworth and her brother joined them.

The expression on Mr. Christian Vanderworth's face was noncommittal, even distant, although he responded politely to their greeting. Kat noticed Mariah's eyes brighten, just as they had earlier at the mention of his name. Surely her sister could not be caught at last by this American! Casting a worried glance at Lady Tutwilliger, Kat was relieved to see her dear godmother seemed totally unaware of Mariah's enraptured countenance.

"Yes, Miss Vanderworth, Lord Thistlewait was *so* disappointed he could not be in attendance tonight," Lady Tutwilliger twittered. "He particularly asked us to relay his regrets to you, my dear."

Helen Vanderworth blushed a rosy pink and glanced down. "Thank you, Lady Tutwilliger. Lord Thistlewait honors me." Then she looked up, her eyes as bright as Mariah's. "We will miss him tonight, for he does so add to a gathering, does he not?"

With a sinking feeling in her chest, Kat acknowledged that poor Miss Vanderworth had joined the ranks of women bowled over by her twin's disgustingly beautiful looks. Even though the three of them possessed the Thistlewait aquamarine eyes and the Thistlewait dimples, Jacko's eyes were more startling and his dimples deeper. Kat's hair was golden blond, but Jacko's was brighter, more

13

full of light, as if constantly kissed by the sun. It had proved to be a fatal combination. His only saving grace, Kat grudgingly acknowledged, was that he was completely oblivious to the effect his appearance had on the fair sex.

"I believe we are to enter the salon for the concert now." Mr. Christian Vanderworth's voice was cultured and, admittedly, there was a definite air about him as he offered his arm to Lady Tutwilliger.

"Please, Mr. Vanderworth, escort your sister and Lady Mariah. I must have a private word with Kathryn."

Kat watched the three of them comfortably conversing as they crossed the room, and she was left with her fuming godmother.

"Where *is* your reticule?" Lady Tutwilliger demanded.

"Oh! I must have left it with my cloak," Kat sighed, knowing what was coming next.

"When are you going to grow out of this childish habit of misplacing your belongings? Mark my words, it will place you in the suds one of these days. Go fetch it. And keep an eye out for your dreadful twin. He may be lurking about somewhere, the *wretch*!"

Poor Jacko was in for it, but he would talk Willy around, Kat knew. Their godmother was no more proof against Jacko's charm than any other woman, except his long-suffering sisters, of course.

Escaping Lady Tutwilliger's wrath, Kat slowly made her way through each salon, even going so far as to peek into the card room. Several gentlemen had already found their way there and settled in for a fine evening of cards, far away from the Italian soprano

14

Lady Sefton had engaged to entertain the ton. Unfortunately, Jacko was not among them.

A little further down the hall Kat pushed open an antechamber door and stopped, swallowing down a gasp.

"I am so very sorry," she stammered, shocked to find a couple sitting too closely together upon a low couch.

The gentleman's pallid eyes flickered briefly before he stood. "This room is occupied," he announced in an oily voice.

Kat hastily backed up but refused to shut the door completely. The girl had not turned her face away quickly enough; Kat recognized her—Caroline Strange, a young and, word had it, wealthy heiress. Kat also recognized the girl's companion—Sir Edmund Trigge, an out-and-out fortune hunter. Where was Miss Strange's chaperon? Who would allow her to keep company with an older man who possessed such an unsavory reputation?

Kat's nearly overwhelming desire to linger in the hallway and give young Miss Strange some well-meaning advice was squelched by remembering Lady Tutwilliger's warning that above all she must be circumspect this Season. Best not to get involved, Kat decided. It was difficult to walk away because obviously Caroline Strange was as guileless as dear Jacko.

She wrinkled her nose in distaste as the soprano tried, unsuccessfully, to reach a particularly high note. Kat sighed deeply, the sacrifices she had to make for Society!

A footman suddenly appeared at her side, "Lady Kathryn, I believe?" He presented a letter upon a small silver tray.

Her smile quickly vanished as she recognized Jacko's untidy scrawl. Retiring to a bench half-hidden by a large potted plant, Kat opened her brother's note and read.

"Oh, no!" she breathed, hardly able to comprehend her twin's misguided reasoning. Fed up with Lady Tutwilliger's matchmaking he was off to the Continent. But, happily, he had met up with his bosom friends, Mr. Gladstone Pennington and Sir Percy Allendale, and they were all first attending a mill on Berkshire Road. He was putting up at the Blue Boar Inn with the quaintest old lady, a gypsy princess. Kat was not to worry. It was all quite a lark. He wished she could join him.

She folded the note over in her hand. Lady Tutwilliger would never forgive this! What could she do? Dear, sweet, gorgeous Jacko was sure to fall into a scrape without her guidance!

Kat had always been the leader; the consequence of arriving in the world five minutes ahead of John Charles, Lord Thistlewait, heir to Thistlewait Hall, Thistlewait Manor, and the Grange.

What to do about this coil? Kat rapidly rejected the idea of confronting her godmother or Mariah with Jacko's latest wild flight. Somehow she would have to prevent this.

The tall clock in the hallway chimed the hour, and Kat looked up, surprised to realize it was really still quite early. Early enough for her to save the day.

Rising slowly to her feet, Kat brushed a hand across her brow and theatrically tottered toward Lady Sefton's major domo, who stood at rigid attention in the entryway.

"Please call my carriage and relay the message

to Lady Tutwilliger that I have developed a headache and returned home," Kat said breathlessly.

He was solicitation itself; it was all Kat could do to keep him from fetching her godmother immediately to her side. By the time she was safely leaning against the squabs of the carriage, there truly was a naggy ache behind her eyes.

Lady Tutwilliger's butler, Westley, so far forgot himself upon finding her alone on the doorstep that he paled.

"Miss Kathryn! I do trust nothing's amiss," he gasped.

So much for the slight hope that the servants did not realize how tenuous was the Thistlewait hold on a successful Season.

"No, Westley, I simply returned with an unfortunate headache." She sighed deeply, forcing herself to walk ever so slowly toward the stairs. "Please inform my maid I shall not need her until late tomorrow morning. I do not want to be disturbed."

"As you wish, Miss." He bowed, and Kat felt remorse at the true concern on his face and in his voice.

Nevertheless, the moment she was around the first turn in the upper hall, and out of sight, she gathered up the folds of her skirt in one hand and raced toward the room Jacko used upon his too infrequent stays at Tutwilliger House.

Kat had nearly obtained her goal when a door opened; Hannah Hamilton, holding aloft a single candle, stepped into the hallway.

"Kathryn, my dear child! What is wrong?" In the dim light, Hannah's face was ghostlike as if she were badly frightened.

17

Swaying to a sudden stop, Kat smiled weakly. "Dear Hannah, I am so sorry if I gave you a start. I have simply returned with a headache. All I need is a nice long sleep."

"But, dear, your room is not down this hall," Hannah breathed, her forehead wrinkling into several worried lines.

"Yes, but ... but I was in Jacko's room earlier and left a book of poems. ... I ... I thought perhaps I would read before retiring," Kat finished triumphantly, surprised at how quickly she could come up with the white lie.

"But, Kathryn, reading will surely not improve your headache." Hannah's worry dissolved into the glazed look that came over her whenever she realized she might be in the midst of a conflict.

"I assure you I shall be quite all right tomorrow, Hannah," Kat said softly and yawned conspicuously. "Perhaps you should make an early night of it yourself."

"Yes, perhaps you are right." Yawning delicately, Hannah backed into her room. "I suddenly feel the need for a rest myself. Good night, dear."

As soon as the door shut Kat looked quickly both ways down the hall to make sure no one else was about before she bolted into Jacko's room and locked the door behind her.

Everything she needed was right there.

Chapter 2

WHATEVER HAD POSSESSED him to attend the mill on Berkshire Road, Jules did not know. But he had gone, and he had bet, and he had won a considerable sum on the winning pugilist. Now he was more than a little foxed, back at the Blue Boar Inn surrounded by three young twigs of the ton. They were deliriously happy for his success, giving no thought whatsoever to their own losses.

"Here, Saville, try this brandy. Quite good stuff," his new acquaintance, John Thistlewait, slurred, and slid a glass across the table.

Jules tipped the brandy down his throat, its warmth spreading in languorous fingers through his body. He nodded. "Excellent, Thistlewait. Now, I really should make an early night. I'm for the coast at dawn."

"Damn it, Count, just getting to be friends! Impressed with your knowledge of pugilism." The young lord gave him a roguishly dimpled smile. "Penny and Percy ain't no company tonight. They're otherwise occupied."

He was correct, his friends were both fawning over the serving wench. Mr. Gladstone Pennington, cravat twisted beneath his right ear, looked ready to pass out, but Sir Percy Allendale was sober enough to hold the wench firmly upon his lap.

Jules found Pennington and Allendale to be good enough fellows, although he had a suspicion Sir Percy was a sad rattle. Thistlewait he particularly liked. Probably because the youngster reminded Jules of his brother, Dominic, when he was young.

So, Jules took another long draught of brandy and prepared to discuss the mill in greater detail with the eager young lord and his friends.

Berkshire Road proved a greater distance than Kat had anticipated. No sound, except her horse's rhythmic hoofbeats, broke into the darkness. Every mile brought a new doubt. Had she taken the right action? She had to pull it off now, and be back before anyone missed her. It might be fun to meet a real gypsy—if indeed the inn's proprietress was one. Shouldn't she be there by now? Jacko's note! She hoped she stuffed it away somewhere. Oh well, no one would think to look in Jacko's room until she was safe again in London with her twin beside her.

Kat caught her breath, half-faint with relief when the low hanging moon finally lit the Blue Boar Inn's wooden sign.

She leapt from the saddle, tossing her reins to the postboy. Lowering her voice, she forced a cough. "Rub him down and give him an extra bag of oats," she mumbled, flipping the boy a coin. Instantly he did as he was bidden without the blink of an eye. The first hurdle was crossed.

Adjusting her greatcoat and drawing herself to her full height, Kat entered the inn. Male laughter, loud and cheery, greeted her from the taproom. Pulling her hat a bit farther down her forehead, she peered carefully through the open rectangle. A low fire burned merrily in the grate and comfortable-looking high-backed chairs were placed around square tables, most of which were littered with empty bottles.

Thank goodness he was here! The nagging doubt that she would really be in the suds if she somehow missed him was removed. It was more of a relief than she imagined.

Penny and Percy were making fools of themselves over some serving girl who was more out of her low-cut blouse than in it. A peal of Jacko's laughter drew her eyes to another table in a shadowy corner. There he was, her twin, happy as a lark, conversing with great animation to some gentleman who had his back to Kat. He didn't seem at all familiar. All she could tell was that the stranger had raven black hair and broad shoulders.

What to do? She couldn't simply rush into the room and confront her errant twin.

"May I be of assistance?"

Kat whirled around at the crisp inquiry. A tiny woman with a worn brown face and grizzly white hair pulled up into an enormous bun confronted her. Could this be Jacko's gypsy princess?

"My lord, I didn't recognize you at first. Didn't realize you'd gone out again." The innkeeper's sharp eyes slowly surveyed the greatcoat that hung loosely upon Kat's shoulders.

Shifting it back into place, Kat again drew herself up as tall as possible. "Think I'm coming down with something," she mumbled as gruffly as she could. "Felt a bit chilly."

Kat was not surprised by the old woman's skeptical smile. It was actually quite unseasonably warm.

"Lord Thistlewait, I shall have a hot punch sent to your room at once."

"My room?" Kat questioned. "Yes, of course, my

21

room," Kat muttered self-consciously, backing toward a narrow winding staircase. "I will retire to my room."

Kat could feel the older woman's eyes on her as she hesitated on the landing, studying six closed doors.

"Third on the right, my lord," the innkeeper called.

Kat nodded, then coughed several more times. "Send that hot punch right along," she demanded gruffly, before escaping into the safety of Jacko's room.

The flames from the fireplace and a three-branch candelabrum on the bedside table lit the cozy low-ceilinged chamber. The bed, already turned down for the night, looked inviting; the linen felt freshly clean when Kat ran her palm over it. Lavender. The innkeeper had rinsed it in lavender, and the delicate scent permeated the pillows and sheets.

Kat straightened with a start when a short knock heralded the old woman's entrance; she carried a tray containing a steamy mug of appealing brew.

"Here you are, my lord," she said briskly, setting the tray beside the bed. "This should do the trick."

"Thank you," Kat muttered, trying to move deeper into the corner of the room. Again she was subjected to a quizzical appraisal of her slightly strange attire. "Thank you again, ma'am. That shall be all. Good night," Kat finished firmly.

With an almost regal nod, the innkeeper left the room, closing the door quietly behind her.

What could she do? Kat really had no other choice but to wait for her twin to come up. She fervently hoped the raven-haired gentleman did not keep Jacko too long; they had a tiresome journey back to London ahead of them tonight. Even with Jacko to chaperon her, she'd have a hard time explaining her presence here.

Gratefully sliding out of the unwieldy coat, the only garment she could find in Jacko's closet big enough to conceal her true identity, she sat on the bed. It didn't take long to remove the Hessians; they were way too big for her. She'd had to stuff old darned stockings in the toes to keep them on. The neckcloth was tossed, with the greatcoat, onto the chair in the dark corner. Taking a deep breath, she tightened her stomach and undid Jacko's breeches.

What a relief! It had been a few years since she'd dressed up in her brother's clothes to fool their friends. Last time the breeches had not fit so snugly. The lawn shirt also pulled across her bosom so she slid several buttons open. Perhaps Jacko's clothes no longer fit because she was finally developing some curves like Mariah.

Much more comfortable, she leaned back upon the pillows. The enticing aroma from the mug tempted her to lift it to her lips. She was most definitely parched from her journey. The punch was surprisingly smooth going down. In fact, it was so soothing that she drank the entire contents of the mug.

Suddenly her eyelids felt ridiculously heavy. It couldn't hurt to close her eyes and take the tiniest rest while waiting for Jacko.

Snuffing out the candles, she settled back upon the soft pillows. Really, it was amazing how tired she suddenly felt; all her former apprehension about Jacko slowly dissolved into a blissful peace.

Jules found the steps shockingly uneven; his boots kept slipping off of them. Strange, he had not noticed that before. Nor had he noticed how many blasted doors there were in this inn's hallway. Carefully he counted, his room was the third . . . on the left.

"Saville!"

Jules whirled to turn back and peer over the banister. The hall pitched and spun wildly before coming into focus. Lord John Thistlewait, his golden curls tumbling about his flushed face, stared up at him. He waved the brandy bottle.

"Saville, we have yet to finish."

"You go ahead without me," Jules encouraged. "I will take my leave of you tomorrow."

With a small salute and another dimpled smile, Lord Thistlewait turned to stagger back into the tap room.

Taking a deep breath and finding that it did not clear his rather befuddled mind, Jules looked to the third door. Yes, he most definitely needed a good night's sleep before continuing his journey to the coast. He was past the age of drinking contests with the young bucks downstairs.

The low-ceilinged room was in darkness except for a small yellow light from the dying embers of the fireplace. Where were the damn candles? The innkeeper should have provided more light than this. Too tired to fuss, Jules felt for the side of the bed and sat gingerly. Not being at his absolute best, and not having the benefit of a valet, he struggled with his Hessians, swearing softly in French.

Pushing himself to his bare feet he tore off his shirt, tossing it to the floor. He fumbled with several of his trouser buttons, but was only half-finished when he gave up in disgust. Lying back on a pillow he slowly shut his eye. He hadn't been this far gone since Oxford.

Which was why, at first, he thought perhaps he

24

was hallucinating when his chamber door burst open and the room suddenly filled with lights and a veritable crowd of shouting people.

Gwynneth Tutwilliger had never fainted in her life, at least not without careful planning, but at this precise moment she came very close to succumbing to the vapors.

"Kathryn!"

"Saville!" Jacko's roar echoed an instant later.

Both parties sat up on the bed: Kathryn, looking as if her lashes were weighing too heavily upon her lids, her hair tumbling loose from the ribbon that had held it up under her hat, the lawn shirt she wore half-unbuttoned, as were the breeches that molded her curvy thighs. Saville, his straight black hair falling over the patch covering his left eye, his broad shoulders and muscled chest tawny gold in the firelight, his breeches unbuttoned to barely conceal his manhood.

"Saville, what is the meaning of this?" Jacko roared, taking a step forward.

Saville! Lady Tutwilliger's frantic mind latched on to that name. There could only be one Saville who wore a black riband and possessed a scarred cheek: Jules Devereaux, Comte de Saville, the stepgrandson of her old friend, Sybilla, Duchess of Culter.

All was not lost!

Lady Tutwilliger flung out her arms, stopping Jacko's charge toward the bed.

"Saville, we are so *delighted* you were here to assist Lady Kathryn when she fell ill!" Lady Tutwilliger praised, and then twirled to the sea of faces staring at her.

Mariah and Hannah wore the same stricken expression; Jacko's mouth fell open, as did Gladstone

Pennington's. She seared Sir Percy's enthralled face with her most penetrating gaze, the one that had shriveled stronger men than this sad rattle. There was no doubt in her mind if she did not act quickly this would be the on-dit of the ton upon Percy's return to London.

Marshaling her forces, Gwynneth Tutwilliger pushed fate's disaster into an acceptable story that could stand circulation.

"Sir Percy, please ask the innkeeper to send up some strengthening broth for Lady Kathryn. If only one of our horses hadn't thrown a shoe. We would have arrived with Lady Kathryn and dear Jules would not have had to play nursemaid. But you know how impetuous betrothed couples can be."

Sir Percy lifted his brows. "Lady Kathryn and Saville are betrothed?" He had the effrontery to quirk his lip at her.

"But of course!" Lady Tutwilliger narrowed her eyes. "It is of long, albeit, secret, standing."

Under her prolonged gaze he flushed and stepped back. "Of course, my lady. I will order the broth at once."

"Go with you, old boy," Gladstone Pennington sputtered, nearly pushing his friend out the door.

At their exit, Mariah could no longer contain herself. She rushed, tears streaming down her pinkened cheeks, to her sister's side and threw a protective arm about her shoulders. Hannah took advantage of the moment and tottered to a small chair in front of the fireplace where she promptly closed her eyes. Jacko impatiently pushed past his godmother to confront the Comte de Saville, who had taken these few moments to redon his lawn shirt, thereby concealing one of the most attractive

26

chests Lady Tutwilliger had ever had the good fortune to glimpse.

"Sorry for it, Saville. Liked you, but it must be pistols at dawn," Jacko stated grimly.

The chorus of feminine shrieks effectively cleared the paralyzing shock that had descended upon Jules since all bedlam had broken loose in his bedchamber.

"Wretched boy, you can't duel with your sister's intended!" shrieked the harridan in the lilac turban.

The mousy woman in the chair opened her eyes only long enough to breathe, "But, Jacko, you are such a bad shot," before closing them again.

The little beauty with the dark curls stamped her foot. "Jacko, you can't hit the broad side of the barn! I won't let you do it!"

"Of course he's not going to duel!" declared Lady Kathryn, scrambling to her knees to cast them all a pleading look. "There has been a terrible mistake!"

For the first time Jules took a good look at the reason for all of this lunacy. She was the spitting image of Lord John Thistlewait, except upon more careful examination Jules saw there was a softness about her skin and features that clearly proclaimed her a female. He could see she could easily pass for her brother if she covered the swelling breasts clearly discernible through the fine lawn shirt and concealed the way the breeches curved over her hips and thighs. More often than not, people saw what they expected to see. Obviously she had passed for Lord Thistlewait tonight and somehow had gotten into the wrong room.

"Your sister is correct, Thistlewait. Obviously she is in the wrong room."

"This is the right room! You are in the wrong

room at the wrong time!" declared the dark-haired beauty whose flashing aquamarine eyes branded her another Thistlewait. "Now that sad rattle Sir Percy will spread this tale, and my dear Kat will be ruined, all because of you!"

"Now, Mariah, calm yourself," the purple turban soothed. She looked squarely at Jules. "Saville, *I* am Lady Tutwilliger, godmother and only guardian to the Thistlewait children. I'm sure we can effectively squelch any nasty rumors by announcing your engagement to Kathryn in the *Gazette*."

He sent her his most quelling stare. "This is eighteen nineteen, not the dark ages, ma'am. No one can force anyone to marry." Transferring his gaze to Lord John Thistlewait, he stared into the young, flushed face. "I barely left you more than a quarter of an hour ago. Hardly time to dishonor your sister."

Jacko in turn looked at his sister whose pleading face was his undoing. He shook his head, shrugging. "What's to do, Saville? Damn coil if you ask me."

"I know what must be done," Lady Tutwilliger insisted, thrusting up her bosom that tested her lilac satin gown to its limits. "And I am sure my old friend, Sybilla, Duchess of Culter, will share my feelings."

A chill settled over Jules, effectively banishing the last lingering effects of the alcohol he'd consumed. "You know my stepgrandmother?"

"*Know* her! We have been friends since our come-out together forty years ago. She has written me most glowingly of your half brother, the Marquis of Aubrey, and the new baby. Giles! Yes, that is your nephew's name, is it not?"

Jules threw up his head arrogantly and returned Lady Tutwilliger's stare. "Yes, that is my nephew's name. You know my family well."

"But of course," Lady Tutwilliger graced him with a wide smile. "So well that I feel sure Sybilla will be delighted that you will be following your brother into the blissful state of matrimony. Such a much more pleasant expectation than the whispers of scandal."

Jules feared nothing and no one, for he had faced his darkest hour and survived. He did not fear scandal for himself, but he would do nothing to mar Dominic's happiness, nor cause pain to the duke and duchess. They had stood by him through much and were his only family.

"Willy, what are you about?" Lady Kathryn gasped, nearly falling off the bed in her eagerness to rush to her godmother's side. "Stop this at once!" She cast pleading looks at her siblings, but Jacko glanced away sheepishly, probably glad to be spared an otherwise inescapable duel, and Mariah bowed her head, although Jules could see how she shook with sobs. Finally the lady turned to him. "My lord, please make them all understand!"

Jules met Lady Kathryn's impassioned stare with an appraising one of his own.

She was tall for a woman and possessed a willowy figure that promised riper curves to come. Her golden hair curled in wild exuberance about her beautiful face, and her heavily lashed aquamarine eyes were wide. In their depths he saw fear. This child was as ingenuous as she appeared.

Jules gave her a brief, reassuring smile. "Lady Tutwilliger, I wish a few moments alone with Lady Kathryn."

Kathryn looked stunned at the audacity of the request, but her godmother nodded readily. "I, of course, cannot allow you to be alone in this bedchamber. Hannah shall chaperon. Come along, Mariah. Jacko."

Like a mother hen she guided her charges toward the door. Mariah appeared ready to disobey, then gave her sister a long hug before rushing from the room.

"You have five minutes," Lady Tutwilliger declared before, head erect, turban plume waving, she swept out the door.

Jules glanced warily toward Hannah sitting so quietly before the fire.

"You may speak freely. She is asleep," Kathryn stated dully.

And indeed a soft, tentative snore issued forth from that corner.

Jules could not help smiling. What a hornet's nest he had tumbled into. He was a man who had seen and done much worse. On the journey here he had mused that his future lay before him. Apparently he had opened the wrong door and found it.

He stopped in stunned surprise, remembering Mrs. Forbes's prophesy . . . *The wrong door shall be the right one for you.* Right or wrong the die was cast.

Taking two steps forward he stared straight into Kathryn Thistlewait's pale, frightened face.

"My dear Lady Kathryn, will you do me the great honor of becoming my wife?"

Chapter 3

KAT WAS NUMB with horror, had been since her entire family burst through the door, and she had discovered herself in bed with a stranger. But his calm acceptance of Lady Tutwilliger's outrageous suggestion restored her natural spirit.

"My lord, that's a terrible idea! We are total strangers!" she argued.

"Lady Kathryn, in the ton, more often than not, strangers readily become betrothed," he answered quietly.

Somehow she must make him see reason! She stared at him. His body was fluid and long. Even though she was not short, his height made him seem to tower above her, and she had to lean back to meet his gaze. The soft firelight revealed raven black hair falling straight across his brow, brushing the top of the patch covering his left eye. Beneath it a faint, white scar swept his high cheekbone to disappear at his temple. His nose was straight, as was his mouth, straight and firm with some strong emotion.

She set her face in equally firm lines and folded her arms across her breasts. "This entire incident is totally, utterly ridiculous! You and I know noth-

31

ing untoward happened between us. We must simply make the rest of them all see reason."

"Your godmother is suggesting the only course she can see that Society will accept. Even so there will be talk. She knows you must have an impeccable reputation to make any marriage, much less an advantageous one." His mouth curved into a flicker of a rueful smile, and his gaze was so intensely brown as to appear black. "The ton is a censorious world."

Kat knew that, had always known it. Growing up a Thistlewait—the child of the lord who had jilted a duke's daughter to run off with his gamekeeper's daughter—insured her early realization of what rumor could do to a life. She was a child of scandal, and only Lady Tutwilliger's power in the ton, plus the fact that the Thistlewaits were connected to half the upper one hundred, made them acceptable. Kat wasn't afraid of censure or scandal; she had already survived it.

Thrusting up her chin, she said as much to the Comte de Saville. "I am not afraid of gossip. I have faced it before."

"Your courage does you credit, *ma petite*. Have you also faced your brother defending your honor?" His voice was tight with frustration. "He will have to call out his friend Allendale to stop the spread of this tale. If he survives that encounter there will be others who will insult you. Your brother will feel honor bound to defend you in the only means possible."

She stepped back, clasping her hand to her suddenly hot throat that had swelled with tears. "Jacko can't duel! He'd be killed," she whispered, realizing just how serious her predicament was. How could her plan to keep Jacko from running off to the continent have ended so disastrously? Instinct demanded she turn and run from this stranger who seemed as determined as Willy upon this absurd course. She whirled about in frustration and pressed her closed fists into her cheeks, seeking desperate inspiration.

"We must not put Jacko in the position of defending you." He continued calmly and, for the first time, a softness sweetened his face. "Lady Kathryn, you do not want this any more than I, but we must agree to avoid an ugly scandal. I realize I am not much of a prize." So saying he flicked one long thin finger over his cheek. "But I am reasonably fixed and an honorable man. I will make you an unexceptional husband."

Kat experienced a jolt of surprise that he should deride himself. She did not think his face unattractive—mysterious, perhaps. Or utterly detached, as if he could pull totally within himself and let nothing or no one reach him. That was not the husband for her. Kat wanted love and laughter, those vague reminiscences of her youth.

"I'm afraid I have no estate in England, but I do have relatives who will always welcome us." He shrugged. "Château Saville is rumored to have been beautiful once. I am on my way to France now to oversee its renovation. Perhaps—"

"But that is of all things wonderful!" Kat interrupted, her mind leaping ahead to the possibilities. "That is the answer to all our problems."

"I beg your pardon, my lady. What is the answer?" he returned quietly, although his right brow was raised in rather a haughty fashion.

"Going to France! Yes, it is perfect!" Kat declared, pacing back and forth in her excitement. "We shall let Willy and the ton think we are engaged. You and I, with Jacko and Hannah, of course, will travel to your château. We will stay a fortnight or so. Then we will find that we do not suit. I shall cry off. Jacko, Hannah, and I shall leave, traveling slowly through the continent, thereby satisfying Jacko's wanderlust. By then Mariah should be happily settled. For you know," she continued confidingly, "this should be her fourth Season. Papa was so ill the year of her come-out she refused to go. Then he died and we were in mourning so we missed a year. Last Season we were presented together, but she refused the duke, so this year she really must . . ."

Kat stopped for breath and looked up to discover the comte's dazed countenance. "I am sorry. You must think me the veriest peagoose. But, truly, I believe this plan might serve both our needs."

He shook his head and moved one step closer. He gave her a real smile, one that turned his mysterious, detached features into something else indeed! He suddenly reminded Kat of every dashing hero in the novels she and Mariah routinely checked out of Hookum's Lending Library.

He took her hand, raised it slowly to his lips, and at his touch breathless excitement fluttered in strange parts of Kat's anatomy.

"Lady Kathryn, I do not think you a peagoose. And I am perfectly willing to hear what your godmother makes of this plan."

"*Plan!* What plan?" Lady Tutwilliger asked from the doorway. She sailed into the room, Jacko and Mariah following in her wake. Even Hannah opened her eyes and sat up, glancing around in renewed attention.

"Willy, I have come up with the perfect solution!" Kathryn exclaimed.

Jules retired to the fireplace to lean one shoulder against the mantel and observe the Thistlewaits in action.

His betrothed, amazingly he already thought of her in that context, outlined her plan of accompanying him to France. But she did fail to mention her intention to cry off. He wouldn't, couldn't, allow her to do that, but he didn't have the heart to tell her just now, immediately after her masterful stratagem. In the end, somehow, he would make her understand this marriage would suit them both. He wasn't quite sure why he had agreed—to keep the scandalmongers from Dominic and his family, who had suffered enough. Yes, he recognized that reason. But there was something more. Jules had truly loved very few people in his life. And certainly after his accident there had been little room in his thoughts for such a soft emotion. But these last months at Culter Towers with his only "family" had exposed yearnings he didn't think he'd possessed.

In his world there were very few love matches like Dominic and Juliana. He couldn't hope for one, so this arrangement with Kathryn Thistlewait would suit was well as any. He could, after all, have a semblance of happiness and family for himself. Besides, he admitted, he was rather fascinated by this unusual young woman with the undeniable streak of daring.

To Jules's surprise, Lady Tutwilliger didn't immediately begin a tirade at the idea of their journey to France. Instead she eyed her charge sternly. "It might well be just the thing. A family wedding at the Saville ancestral estate, only recently restored to its owner." She considered briefly, her lilac plume nodding in rhythm with one tapping finger. "Charming."

"Not be at Kat's wedding!" Mariah wailed, rushing to her sister's side to embrace her.

"No, Mariah, do not be upset," Kathryn soothed. "It will be all right, never fear."

Lady Tutwilliger fixed Jules with a cool stare. "Well, Comte, we have yet to hear from you regarding this plan."

"I am at the disposal of my betrothed's wishes," he uttered, bowing and meeting Kathryn's truly remarkable eyes. Fear no longer lurked there, instead there was a glimmer of determination and, yes, excitement. He was just beginning to understand this willowy beauty had the heart of an adventurer.

Suddenly he needed to know one fact. "I ask only one question. Does our arranged marriage keep Lady Kathryn from going where her heart dictates?"

Every eye in the room turned to Kathryn. She didn't seem to notice. She returned his gaze steadily, her beautiful eyes clear and wide. "My heart is my own, Monsieur le Comte," she answered quietly.

Oddly, Jules's heart gave one strong thud and he had to take a deep breath before it began, again, to beat normally.

"Then, my dear, we are for France."

Gwynneth Tutwilliger settled more deeply into the blue velvet pillows of her traveling coach, extremely relieved it was so well sprung. She was utterly and completely exhausted. The Thistlewait children were a handful, but they were as dear to her as if they were her own. Actually, she thought of them as hers, for their own mother, Bettina, had died when the twins were only five, and she had more or less had the rearing of them. When no one else would, she had stood by Francis Thistlewait. But, after all, they had been friends since the cradle. How could she have done any less? She didn't regret a moment. They were scamps, but she adored them and was determined to see them all happily settled.

Another deep sob broke from Mariah that Lady Tutwilliger could ignore no longer.

"What *are* you sniffling about?"

Mariah looked up, her lashes drenched with tears. "We must go back to the inn. You cannot sacrifice Kat on the altar of respectability. Her romantic nature will never survive a loveless marriage."

Impressed with Mariah's persistent desire to aid her sister, Lady Tutwilliger folded her arms across her ample bosom and gave her an encouraging smile. "What do you suggest, Miss?"

"I shall take Jacko and Kat and retire to the country." She sniffed. "Eventually the scandal will die down. Jacko is such an Adonis, he will, in time, make a brilliant match. Kat will find true love, just as she's always wanted." Another sniff escaped and Mariah dabbed at her eyes with a scrap of lace. "And I . . . I will devote myself to good works!"

"Oh, ho!" laughed the indulgent godmother. "And what about Mr. Vanderworth?"

Mariah paled, staring back at her with the amaz-

37

ing Thistlewait eyes, brightened by strong emotion. "My duty and love for my family is greater than any . . . any slight . . . regard I might have for Mr. Vanderworth." Mariah thrust up her softly rounded chin. "I demand we return to the inn, Willy."

"I've said it before and I'll say it again. You'll all be the death of me! That minx you call sister has no intention of going through with this marriage. But she won't pull a fast one on me. I shall send a missive straight away to dear Sybilla. That can be a formidable family, when united. The comte will do the proper and Kat will have no say in it."

Mariah stared at her in horror. "Willy, how can you be so cruel? Kat intends to marry for love like Mama and Papa."

Too good-hearted to bear any more of Mariah's sobs, Lady Tutwilliger leaned over and patted her hands. "Buck up, my dear. Did you get a good look at the comte? Never saw a man more cut out to be a girl's romantic hero. Kat will be head over heels in love with the handsome rogue in no time or my name isn't Gwynneth Euterpe Frogmorton Tutwilliger!"

Chapter 4

Kᴀᴛ ꜰʟᴜɴɢ ʙᴀᴄᴋ her head to breathe in the salty air of the English Channel. She loved the sea; there was a dichotomy that appealed to her senses—the regular rhythms of the tide versus the sudden violent storms. She could hardly believe she was here on a packet to France, supposedly on her way to being married. Married to a stranger purely because they had spent five minutes together upon the same bed by accident. It was utterly ridiculous! She did not feel the tiniest bit guilty that she had fibbed to Willy. Well, perhaps the tiniest bit, particularly when their trunks had been waiting for them on the wharf, just as Lady Tutwilliger had promised, and with them, a note from her godmother that made Kat slightly misty eyed. She would make it up to dear Willy somehow. But she simply could not wed where she did not love.

"Lady Kathryn, I trust the accommodations are satisfactory for you and Miss Hamilton."

She turned to face the man the world thought her intended husband. The fresh damp air of the channel had coiled its fingers through his dark hair so now it no longer fell straight across his forehead, but bent in the slightest wave near his riband.

"Quite satisfactory, thank you, Monsieur le

Comte. Miss Hamilton has already retired for the duration of the crossing. She does not care for ships or water or travel."

"But you do?" he inquired, lifting that right brow which made his thin face look positively saturnine.

"Yes, I love it! The idea of sailing to far-off places, seeing new sights. It is such an adventure!" She laughed with the pure excitement of it, then suddenly realized she was perhaps saying more than she should. "Lady Tutwilliger feels that I am perhaps a trifle too adventuresome," she added in what she hoped was a demure tone.

"Does she really?" he asked cordially; and although Kat could see nothing but polite interest on his face, she most definitely had heard a thread of laughter in his voice. She wasn't surprised. No doubt he thought them all mentally deranged. He was as caught in this coil as she, and he was being remarkably forbearing to go along with her idea. Although in the end, he would also be free of their unfortunate entanglement.

As Kat had done throughout her life, she faced this crisis honestly. "My lord, I don't know why you are being so kind as to go along with my plan." She smiled. "But I promise I shall be as little trouble as possible, and as soon as we can reasonably depart from Château Saville, we shall. You may think all the Thistlewaits are to let in their attics, but I promise you all will end well."

"Lady Kathryn, I think the Thistlewaits delightful, and I, too, believe this all will end well." He gave her, just as he had in the bedchamber of the Blue Boar Inn, a real smile, one that warmed his dark gaze to chocolaty brown and once again caused

40

visions of romantic heroes to flit through her thoughts.

"Then we understand one another," Kat said firmly and gratefully.

The comte's stare seemed particularly piercing to Kat as he reached for her hand. "Lady Kathryn, I—"

Hands suspended in midair, they were suddenly separated by Jacko. He rushed up out of nowhere effectively shutting off their moment of intimacy. "Sorry, Saville. Must borrow my sister."

Kat could do no more than nod as Jacko hurried her off. She experienced a faint disappointment that he had not been able to finish his sentence. Certainly it would be more comfortable for all concerned if everything were firmly settled between them. Jacko dragged her below to the narrow passageway.

"Jacko, what is—?" She was cut rather abruptly off by her brother's hand over her mouth.

"Listen!" he whispered urgently, motioning his head to the door behind her.

Straining her ear to the wooden panel, Kat caught the unmistakable sobs of a woman.

She gently pushed her brother's palm from her face. "It is a girl crying."

"Saw them board. Couldn't see the girl's face. Wrapped in a hooded cloak. But saw him. Sir Edmund Trigge. Man's such a bounder, wouldn't put kidnapping past him."

Kat recognized the fire in her twin's eyes, so like her own. They had always shared the one common passion: be it bringing home wounded birds for the groom to nurse or collecting stray kittens, once they'd even tried to introduce a baby skunk into

41

the household. They just couldn't turn away from any creature in need.

Just the other night, Kat had really had to fight all her instincts, and had left that girl—

"Heavens, Caroline Strange!" Kat gasped, suddenly realizing who was probably behind the door. "Jacko, where is Sir Edmund?"

"Taking a turn on deck. Saw him when I was looking for you and Saville."

"Keep watch on the stairs. Whistle a warning if he returns. I'm going to find out what's going on here," she whispered, shooing him to his post before knocking.

"Miss Strange ... Miss Strange, it is Lady Kathryn Thistlewait. Please let me in. I can help you," she stated calmly and clearly, showing a confidence she wasn't quite sure she possessed.

She sighed in relief and stepped back when eager fumblings on the inside proved the door would be opened to her. Two red-rimmed periwinkle blue eyes peeked out through a small crack.

"Are you alone?" uttered a breathless little voice.

At Kat's nod the door creaked open just enough for her to slip through and then immediately slammed shut, Caroline Strange pushing the bolt firmly into place. The face she turned to Kat was drained of all color except for red swollen patches showing a bout of recent weeping.

"You must help me!" she pleaded before throwing herself, sobbing, into Kat's arms.

Caroline Strange was so tiny, even more diminutive than Mariah, so Kat felt a veritable amazon beside her. Her protective instincts aroused to a fever pitch, Kat led the hysterical girl to the bed and seated her, keeping a reassuring arm around her.

"You must stop crying so. Here, take my hand-kerchief." Kat soothed. "Yes, that's right. Dry your eyes so we may talk."

"My life is over," uttered Caroline, her huge, ter-rified, blue eyes filling her pale face.

Dread filled Kat's heart. What had the bounder done to this poor girl? "Start at the beginning," she encouraged, patting Caroline's hands where they tugged nervously on the damp handkerchief.

"You saw us that night at Lady Sefton's. Sir Ed-mund proposed."

"Good god, how dare he! Where was your chaperon? Tell me how this came about," Kat demanded gently.

"Oh! My papa was a nabob, you know, and when he died two years ago his solicitor, Sir George Bar-tholomew, became my guardian. But Sir George never leaves Northumberland, so he sent me for my come-out to his cousin's, Mrs. Appleton's, who is related to the Earl of Lester. But I do not believe she likes me over much for she lets me go and come as I please."

Such wanton disregard for this young girl's rep-utation fairly made Kat's blood boil. "Then she did not discourage you from seeing Sir Edmund?"

"On the contrary, she encouraged me. I . . . I be-lieve she wished me off her hands. I tried to do the best I could, but I don't know London Society very well. And, oh, Sir Edmund can be very nice when he wishes. I thought I was lucky to catch his no-tice—him being so much older and wiser." At this a new wave of weeping overcame Caroline so it was some few minutes before Kat could encourage her to go on.

"Why are you here, on board this ship for France? He . . . he didn't *kidnap* you, did he?"

Hiccupping, Caroline shook her head. "It is worse. We are eloping."

Aghast, Kat could only sit in stunned silence.

"I know I am beyond redemption," Caroline sobbed. "But it seemed so romantic! He said he couldn't wait to make me his bride. But I am beginning to see it is my fifty thousand pounds a year he cannot wait to make his own." Burying her face in her palms, Caroline gave in to a fit of uncontrollable weeping.

Kat consoled the younger girl as best she could; all the while her mind was searching wildly about for a solution to Caroline's predicament. Kat herself had a broken engagement, but a broken elopement . . . when Caroline had been alone with that man . . . simply was not . . .

It was so simple Kat laughed out loud.

Caroline raised her tear drenched face in shock to stare at Kat in bewilderment.

"Did you leave a note?" Kat asked urgently.

"Yes, I told Mrs. Appleton I was going home to Northumberland."

"Wonderful! That will do nicely. Then when we arrive in Calais, my chaperon, Miss Hamilton, shall send a missive to Mrs. Appleton informing her your plans have changed. You have gone to a house party at the Château Saville with your dear friend, Lady Kathryn Thistlewait. A similar note shall be dispatched to Sir George."

"You would do this for me?" A brilliant smile lit her heart-shaped face, still Caroline Strange looked like a wilted angel. "But I hardly know you."

"Believe me, my dear, I understand your predicament and am happy to be of assistance. Besides, I will enjoy your company. Hurry now, we must be gone before Sir Edmund returns. Do you have any belongings?"

Slipping off the bed, Caroline grabbed a small satchel. "This is all I have," she said, with new animation just bursting forth on her face.

"Good. Come." Kat unlocked the door, and taking her hand, led Caroline out into the corridor. They had only taken two steps when Kat heard her brother's whistle and, an instant later, Sir Edmund Trigge blocked their way.

The pallid eyes Kat remembered too well from the night of Lady Sefton's flickered over her and stopped to rest on Caroline. She shrunk closer to Kat's side.

"What do we have here?" Sir Edmund asked in an all-too-knowing way.

It was everything Kat could do not to retreat before him; but she stood her ground, secure that Jacko was nearby.

"I am simply fetching my dear friend, Miss Strange, to my cabin where she will be more comfortable," Kat answered firmly, thrusting up her chin.

Edmund Trigge was not overly tall so they were very nearly eye to eye. Kat saw his gaze narrow thoughtfully. He glanced around and dismissed Jacko, standing a little behind him, as if he were of no consequence.

"There is some mistake. Miss Strange is my guest," he said smoothly, reaching out one pale hand toward Caroline who was clinging tightly to Kat's arm.

"It's you who's mistaken, Trigge," Jacko snapped, shoving in front of him. "Miss Strange is with my party."

Rigid with indignation, Edmund returned Jacko's

45

glare. "You young pup, stay out of this! 'Tis none of your affair. Come, Caroline, we shall return to our room."

Jacko moved purposively to block his way.

"Sir, I demand you step aside or answer the consequences!" Edmund hissed bitingly.

There was a moment of stunned silence. Jacko remained in place and motioned his sister to take Caroline and move on. In that instant there was a look on Trigge's scarlet face that made fear congeal in Kat's chest. She braced to fling herself forward between them, but, suddenly Edmund's eyes flickered to a movement behind her and all color drained from his face.

"Saville!" he croaked hoarsely, falling back one pace.

"What a charming gathering," the comte remarked, lifting that devilish eyebrow. "But isn't it a trifle cramped down here? Perhaps we should all adjourn to the salon and finish this discussion."

"There is nothing to discuss," Edmund uttered, recovering somewhat. "Miss Strange is under my care. She must stay with me."

The comte's piercing stare studied each face, finally staying on Kat's. She sent him her most beseeching look, much like the one she had given him in the Blue Boar Inn. Now, as then, there was an answering flicker of a reassuring smile.

"And what does Miss Strange have to say?" the comte asked softly, catching Caroline's terrified eyes in his warm gaze.

Caroline appeared mesmerized for an instant before looking imploringly toward Kat. At her nod, Caroline threw up her head.

"Sir Edmund is mistaken. I am going to the Château Saville with Lady Kathryn and her brother."

"Well, there you have it," the comte remarked softly, striding forward to clear a path and motioning Kat and Caroline through. "Perhaps Miss Strange would like to rest before her tea."

Following the comte's directions Kat moved her charge, whose eyes seemed fixed on her toes, past Edmund.

He stood shaking with rage, fists clenched at his sides and muttered something in a low tone that Kat could not quite make out.

The comte had also heard. "Did you say something, Trigge?" he snapped.

Paling again, Edmund stepped back, making a mocking bow. "Only that we shall meet again, Saville."

"Damn bounder!" Jacko uttered when he'd disappeared up the stairs. "Thought I might have to call him out."

"Jacko, don't be foolish," Kat gasped. Fear for his impetuous nature let unfeigned concern color her tone. The last thing she needed was another scandal. Besides she wasn't sure Edmund Trigge could be relied upon to act with honor and refuse the much younger and less-experienced man's challenge.

"It is all my fault!" Caroline cried, burying her face in Kat's shoulder, dampening her puffed silk sleeve.

Jacko's aquamarine eyes instantly filled with compassion and, contrite, he shuffled his feet. "Dash it, didn't mean to upset her."

"Jacko, we shall take ourselves off and let your sister and Miss Hamilton handle this," the comte ordered before giving an elegant leg to Kat. "However, I believe you and I should meet before dinner, Lady Kathryn."

Kat was filled with chagrin. However was she going to explain to the comte that she had added another member to this rather unorthodox house party?

Sipping at his wine, which was barely tolerable, Jules paced around the small dining cabin. A smile flirted with the corners of his mouth. How had this journey to his ancestral home, which had filled him with some mild trepidation, memory being what it was, turned into such a *divertissement*? He felt like a bear-leader: all these children to watch out for and not one of them with the least bit of sense. And that supposed chaperon! She hadn't appeared above decks once.

What would Juliana and Dominic make of the news that he had wed? Feeling a great rush of affection, Jules thought of his delightful sister-in-law. She would, no doubt, attribute it to her gypsy princess, Mrs. Forbes, and her prophesy.

Jules, however, did not possess a romantic nature; he had simply mistaken the room and fate had stepped in. Now he would have to make the best of it. And the best thing for all concerned was a quick, quiet wedding between himself and Lady Kathryn Thistlewait. All he had to do was make the minx see reason.

That prospect did not appear encouraging at all! His intended bride marched into the room, chin thrust to the ceiling, her remarkable Thistlewait eyes flashing.

"Comte," she stated firmly. "There is nothing you can say that will force me to withdraw my protection from Miss Strange. She goes to Château Saville with us or—"

He raised his palm in the hope of warding off another of her lengthy explanations. "I agree," he said softly.

She closed her mouth, blinking ridiculously long dark eye lashes. "You do?"

"Of course. It is plain that Miss Strange needs our protection. But, perhaps you might give me a few of the particulars?"

Jules sipped slowly at his wine as Kat regaled him with the tale. On the surface he preserved a calm, almost bored demeanor. But, inside he seethed. He knew Sir Edmund Trigge. How anyone could still name him a gentleman was beyond Jules's understanding. Their paths had crossed but once on the Continent, but he had heard many stories about the man before and after that incident. It too had involved a very young, very wealthy, very silly girl. And although Jules had not been in time to preserve the girl's reputation, he had saved her life and made absolutely certain that Trigge had not profited from his dastardly deed. The child's guardian had removed her immediately to the Americas so she could begin a new life.

Trigge had reason to hate him, and Jules knew the man played by no rules. The Contessa Marietta Primavetta had known Trigge, also. What she had ever seen in him Jules would never understand.

The fear in Lady Kathryn's eyes showed clearly when she spoke of Trigge, and she was right to feel so. Once again he had been thwarted; they must all be on guard.

"So you see, it will all work out perfectly," Lady Kathryn finished with a sigh. "When I cry off and we leave your château to return to London, Caroline shall accompany us. Her reputation will be intact. Well, my lord, what do you think?"

49

Looking into her eager face, her golden hair like a halo in the candlelight, her aquamarine eyes wide and glistening with excitement, her red ruby mouth with full lower lip curved in a delicious smile, Jules's immediate thoughts were not fit for Lady Kathryn's ears.

Instead, he answered with a lift of his eyebrow and the flicker of a smile. "I think it will do nicely. But I have one request. Since we are, in the eyes of the world, affianced, could you bring yourself to call me by my name?"

"Jules?" she asked softly, and at his nod she grinned. "You are being ridiculously understanding."

Slowly her grin faded, and he was lost again in her remarkable eyes which grew wide and round in excitement and slanted in amusement. Now they did neither; they were quietly serious.

"My lo . . . Jules, I don't know why you are being so understanding in the midst of this coil, but I do appreciate your kindness." A soft pink flushed her high cheekbones. "I want you to know it is not personal, my crying off. It is just that I am determined to wed only for love, like Mama and Papa." Her cheeks were now a rosy red, matching the ribbons threaded through her hair, holding back its wild exuberance.

She seemed to expect no answer so he did not give one, he simply stood as she left the room.

He had never possessed a romantic nature. He had always been a realist. Now, however, there was the faintest quickening of his pulse as he contemplated how he would change Lady Kathryn's mind.

Chapter 5

GWYNNETH TUTWILLIGER BENT over the writing desk in her bedroom, laboring at her letter. In the basket beside her at least a dozen crumpled sheets bore witness to her struggle.

This missive to Sybilla must be sent by the fastest messenger at dawn tomorrow. The sooner everything was set in motion the sooner her darling Kat would be happily settled. Then she could devote her full attention to Mariah; she had already decided Mr. Vanderworth was perfection itself. Gwynneth now had only to make the young man accept that Mariah was his ideal.

Looking down at the lines she had just written Gwynneth groaned aloud. What balderdash! She and Sybilla had been friends for years despite the fact they were both known to be shockingly outspoken. So, she might as well remain true to form and be herself.

Taking a fresh sheet of paper, Gwynneth stuck the quill pen in the ink pot one last time.

"Dearest Sybilla. Come at once. Your stepgrandson, Jules, must wed my godchild, Kathryn Thistlewait, immediately! Fondest regards, Gwynneth."

There! She sat back with a satisfied sigh. *That* should do the trick. With any luck, her godchildren would arrive at Château Saville only a few days before Gwynneth would spring her surprise.

The fiacre Saville had hired was surprisingly well sprung. Even the interior was most comfortable with an abundance of pillows and blankets. Kat had settled Miss Hamilton cozily on one seat while she and Caroline shared the other. The men rode beside them. Kat could see them both out her window: Saville astride his black stallion, brought over on the boat with them from England, and Jacko on a rich chestnut gelding, hired at the last moment.

Saville turned, smiling, to say something to Jacko and Kat was struck by the strength of his profile. From this angle he did not appear detached, as if he were hiding a secret, he appeared to be a man of character and nobility, a man she could depend on and trust. Perhaps it was only the patch that made him appear so unapproachable.

"I know it is vulgarly curious, my lady, but just how did the Comte de Saville lose his sight?" Caroline asked, straining to see out the window.

Caroline was slowly recovering from her fright with what, Kat realized, must be her natural exuberance, so she overlooked the impertinent question. As Kat was Saville's fiancée it was only natural the young girl would think her privy to such information.

"We have never discussed it." Kat smiled. "It is not a matter of any importance to me."

"Oh, how romantic!" Caroline sighed. "To be so in love his scars are as nothing to you! No doubt he earned them bravely in war against that horrid Napoleon creature."

"Yes, I agree with Caroline," Miss Hamilton yawned delicately. "You must inquire, Kathryn, if he was on the Peninsula or at Waterloo. I recall hearing that his brother, the Marquis of Aubrey, distinguished himself." Hannah closed her eyes and then just as quickly lifted her lids. "Or, of course, he could have been maimed in a duel."

A loud gasp escaped Caroline's pursed pink lips. "Never say so, Miss Hamilton! Oh, surely not a duel."

"I think not," Kat answered, shaking her head and glancing back out the window.

The men were laughing, the sunlight accenting their ebony and golden heads. They appeared to get on very well. Jules was a good example for Jacko, Kat thought. She wouldn't mind at all if her twin emulated the older man.

But all this talk of duels terrified her. She would never have allowed Jacko to call Saville out for her sake—although she was now certain he would not have accepted the challenge—for even if her twin was the youngest member of the Four Horseman's Club, he was the worst swordsman and the poorest shot in the ton.

A tremor of fear pulsed through her. She would never forget the look on Sir Edmund's scarlet face when they had thwarted him. What chance would Jacko have in a duel against him?

Giving herself a mental shake, Kat refused to dwell on such horrid thoughts. This was her first journey to the Continent and she fully intended to enjoy the French countryside.

The ravages of war were hidden under the lush

greenery, and the villages had been whitewashed. But occasionally she could spy a man with a wooden peg or an empty sleeve. The war could never be forgotten with these reminders. Kat wondered how they, as English, would be received by Jules's people. Not, of course, that it really mattered for they would only be staying for a short time. Still, it was his homecoming and she would not wish to cast a shadow over it.

Jules had decided not to press forward and had warned her that they would stop overnight at an inn near Reims.

Les Hirondelles looked very much like an English inn; the painted wooden sign with two doves could have been a taproom sign in any English village. But inside the hospitality was very different. There was no private dining room, their party would have to be content to share a board with the locals. Kat found this prospect delightful, a chance to practice her halting French. Obviously Jules had sent instructions ahead for the innkeeper, and carefully following his French, Kat learned that he was delighted to welcome the comte and his party.

"I have ordered us a light fare for tonight. I find it best when traveling," Jules remarked after seating the ladies, Kat at the head, Caroline and Jacko on one side, Miss Hamilton on the other, and sliding himself into a chair at the foot of the table.

"Have you traveled much, my lord?" Caroline inquired, her wide blue eyes bright with curiosity.

"Yes. I have spent ten years on the Continent and in Greece, Miss Strange."

"Oh, how thrilling!" Caroline enthused. "Until I went to London I had never left Northumberland. Were you on the Peninsula?"

"No, that was my brother, the Marquis of Aubrey. I did not take part in the French wars," he returned flatly, and for the first time Kat noticed him absently run one long finger over his scarred cheek.

Caroline cast a startled look at Hannah and then an even more knowing one at Kat. Her enquiring countenance was easily read by all around the table; if Saville had not received his wounds at war, how then?

"Dash it, Miss Strange, regular chatterbox this evening." Jacko laughed easily, very much like a man accustomed to dealing with sisters. "Let's dine in peace. Need some wine to wash the dust away, Saville."

As if on cue two serving girls appeared with bottles and glasses.

Kat was happy to see Caroline did not seem offended at Jacko's words. She merely shrugged and took a tiny sip of wine.

Not by any outward sign did Jules allow that Caroline's prying was disconcerting. He knew his appearance evoked a lot of questions. He was only surprised they had not come much earlier and from Kathryn. She seemed to take his appearance almost as a matter of course, but then he knew she did not intend to go through with the marriage, so perhaps it held little import for her.

He sat back, once again exuding his mysterious and detached air, not yet willing to deal with the interest that he sensed around the table.

Kat suddenly had the most alarming desire to see beneath that facade. Instead, she picked at the omelet with mushroom sauce, the delicious cassoulet, the dish of peas, and the basket piled high with delicate pastries. She could not, however, resist the apple tart.

She had spoken the truth when she told Caroline that Saville's scars were of no concern to her because in all truth they did not distract from his appeal. And Kat realized he did hold a certain appeal for her; not simply because he was showing her such absurd kindness or because they were bonded together in this stratagem to thwart Society's strictures, but for other reasons that she didn't quite understand. It would be necessary to stay at least a fortnight at the château before she cried off. During their time together she determined to learn more about him.

"Kat . . . Kat, stop wool-gathering!" demanded her insensitive twin. "Miss Strange has been asking you to walk in the garden while we have our port."

Kat glanced up to see Jules already standing to assist Caroline and Hannah from the table.

He lifted that particular eyebrow and flashed her a small smile. "Lady Kathryn, are you all right?"

Blinking rapidly, she nodded. "Yes, a walk in the garden will be just the thing before retiring."

Following them from the dining room where Jacko and Saville already had moved to the fireplace with their port, Hannah yawned. "Kathryn dear, would you mind if I failed to join you? I find traveling so exhausting."

"No, Hannah, you go on up. We shan't be long," she called back, rushing to keep up with Caroline who was already out the side door and into a moonlit garden.

"Oh, look at all the stars!" Caroline sighed, twirling around on the crushed rock path. "And there is the most pleasant scent in the air."

"This is an herb garden." Kat bent lower to the

56

plants. "Here are rosemary, thyme, and fennel. Over there I smell mint. The French are much more clever in their use of herbs for cooking."

"Oh, Kathryn, you are so knowledgeable." Even in the pale moonlight Kat could see how woebegone Caroline's little face had become. "No one ever taught me about such things. I don't even know how to plan menus for a household. Sir George's housekeeper always did so and before that, Papa."

Impulsively, Kat gave the smaller girl a hug. "Perhaps when we reach the château I shall be able to give you some pointers."

"Oh, wonderful!" Caroline clapped her hands, suddenly animated again. "You will soon be the mistress of the château so you will be taking inventory of the linens and the kitchen. You can show me just how to go on. Oh, what fun we shall have! But here I am, going on like a chatterbox, just as your brother said!"

"Don't be taken aback by Jacko." Kat smiled. "He is simply accustomed to dealing with me and our sister, Mariah. He is a bit spoiled I'm afraid."

"Oh, he doesn't bother me a bit," Caroline said breezily. "You are all being so kind I would be a poor creature indeed to complain of anything. I'm only happy that we are all so comfortable together and that your brother can treat me like a sister."

In all her twenty years Kat had never heard another female speak so offhandedly of her devastatingly handsome brother. Intrigued, she couldn't help but laugh softly. "You are very unique, Caroline."

"Oh, because I am not enraptured with what an Adonis Lord Thistlewait is?" She sighed, a trifle dramatically, Kat thought, smiling in the darkness. "I believe I prefer older gentlemen."

The smile was quickly wiped from Kat's face at the idea that this young girl might be developing a tendre for Saville. It was a very uncomfortable thought.

"Perhaps that is why I was so foolish with Sir Edmund. But I have learned my lesson." Thrusting her tiny nose into the air, Caroline stared at her with wide serious eyes. "I shall not be so quick again to think myself attached. I will wait until I meet someone like the comte and we fall in love like the two of you."

Kat could not quite meet those wide trusting eyes so she looked down. She discovered, much to her chagrin, that she must have dropped the small reticule that had hung around her wrist.

"I'm such a peagoose," she muttered, glancing around at the shadowy foliage. "Caroline, could you fetch me a lantern or a candle? It seems I have lost my reticule."

"Oh, my, yes. I shall return in a trice." Lifting up the hem of her blue dimity dress, Caroline fairly flew into the inn.

Kat bent over, brushing aside some unruly mint stalks, hoping to spy the small mesh bag. Really, Willy was right. Kat was shockingly careless with her belongings, and this had most definitely gotten her into the suds. If she hadn't left Jacko's note just lying about, Willy wouldn't have followed her, and they all wouldn't be in this shocking coil.

Hearing footsteps on crushed rocks, she straightened, turning.

"How quick . . ." The words died on her lips as fear bounded into her throat, cutting off her sentence.

Blocking the pathway to the inn door was Sir Ed-

58

mund Trigge, the moonlight bathed his angular face in silver and made his pallid eyes glisten.

"So we meet again, Lady Kathryn," he murmured, moving one step closer.

This time Kat did retreat. "What are you doing here, Sir?" she demanded in as strong a voice as she could muster.

"I am simply breaking my journey, just as you are, my dear." His thin lips curved in a crooked smile. "I saw you from the taproom window where I narrowly missed running into Saville. How fortuitous that we should be able to have this private meeting."

"Sir, you go too far. I wish no private meeting with you." Desperately she searched for a way back to the safety of the inn. She had forgotten she was out of England. Here the customs might be different—she should never have remained in the garden alone.

"No. Of course not." He backed away a step.

Kat felt relief lighten the tightness that had strangled her chest until he continued:

"But then, I didn't ask for your interference on the boat, either." He sneered. "You had best get used to our little meetings, Lady Kathryn, I feel sure they will take place with some regularity."

Only a desperate man would insult her so. "I do not believe Saville or my brother will look kindly upon this threat," she returned, drawing herself up to her full height.

He shook his head with a low, rough chuckle. "I saw your face on the ship. You're afraid of me, aren't you, my dear? But then you should be. You have no idea of what I am capable, do you, Lady Kathryn? So, if you know what's good for you and your brother, this conversation will remain our little secret."

"Kat . . . ?" Twirling around Kat looked toward the

inn. Her twin stood there, holding a lantern high above him. "Is someone out there with you, Kat?"

Gasping, Kat turned back but, somehow, Sir Edmund had melted away into the shadows.

"Kat, you shouldn't be out here alone," complained her brother, marching out to join her. "There, there's the blasted reticule right under your nose." Thrusting it into her nerveless fingers, he grasped her arm, leading her back into the light and noise and safety of the inn.

Once inside the door, she looked up into his handsome face. Nothing could happen to him, she wouldn't allow it. Then suddenly she remembered. "Where is Caroline?"

"Boring poor Saville in the dining room. She rushed in as if you had met with a serious mishap. I was halfway down the hall by the time we realized it was nothing. But I came ahead anyway." He tucked her hand in his arm and leaned over confidingly. "Girl's as pretty as a picture but wears you out with her energy. Talks more than you do, Kat."

Throwing her arms around her brother's broad shoulders, Kat buried her face against his chest. "I love you, Jacko," she declared fiercely.

"Love you, too, you ninny," he murmured, patting her back. "Dash it, Kat, what's come over you?"

"Nothing, silly." Laughing, she pushed away, looking up into his flushed face. "Don't be so embarrassed. Twins are allowed such demonstrations of unseemly affection . . . and, you know, twins are also allowed to demand favors. Steel yourself and show Caroline to her room so I might have a few moments alone with Saville."

Jacko's roguish dimples deepened. "So that's how the wind blows. Can't say I'm not pleased. Saville's the best of good fellows." Laughing, he squeezed her fingers. "Willy would have my head for leaving you unchaperoned, but she'll never know, certainly Hannah won't be able to tell her! Can't think why she insisted the old girl had to come along with us."

Saville stopped in midsentence when they entered the room. His penetrating gaze never left Kat's face, not even when, without ceremony, Jacko whisked Caroline off to her bedchamber.

"Something has happened," he stated quietly. "Tell me."

Kat had been fully prepared to throw this new problem upon Saville's broad chest and let him handle it, but it suddenly dawned on her that she didn't wish to place him in any danger, either. After all, she was the one who had interfered with Sir Edmund's dishonorable game.

"I have simply been mulling over the unfortunate events with Sir Edmund on the packet." She forced herself to look at him unblinkingly. "He seemed to know you. Had you met before?"

"Unfortunately, yes. Our paths have crossed. We were in Rome at the same time two years ago. But that is not all you wish to know, is it, Lady Kathryn?"

It was uncanny how quickly this man had learned to read her. Shocked, Kat widened her eyes in an attempt to fob him off. But tears threatened, and apparently she was unsuccessful in diverting him. She heard him utter a small sound before stepping forward.

"My dear Lady Kathryn, we are partners in our little charade, are we not? Let me share whatever is troubling you."

His kindness was her undoing. One tear escaped her control to slide down her cheek. "I am being foolish I know, but the man truly frightens me. The devil you know is better than the devil you do not. Will you pay me the courtesy of being honest? I have placed us all in danger, have I not? He is a ruthless man."

He hesitated, and she could sense he was going to reassure her. "If you please, Jules, I would prefer the truth," she insisted quietly, just the barest quiver in her voice.

"Then you shall have it." Lifting her hand, he held it loosely, soothingly, between his palms. "The rumors of Sir Edmund are not pleasant. For sport as a young buck in London he beat up elderly cits. Later, he lost much of his family fortune gambling. He is cruel, and he can be deadly."

"Deadly? Has he ever killed his man—"

"Blast it, Kat, can't expect Saville to talk about such things with a lady!" roared her brother from the doorway.

Startled, Kat pulled her hand from Saville's warm comforting grip and swung around. "Jacko, what are you doing back here?"

"Thought I should act the chaperon. Your brother, after all," he declared, aquamarine eyes flashing. "Glad I did. You ninnyhammer, can't ask Saville questions like that until you're leg shackled. Could have asked me. Everyone knows Sir Edmund's been on the Continent for years in exile after killing his second man in a duel!"

Kat dared not look at Jules for fear he would see the truth in her eyes. Sir Edmund had been right; their conversation in the garden could be revealed to no one.

Chapter 6

Gᴡʏɴɴᴇᴛʜ Tᴜᴛᴡɪʟʟɪɢᴇʀ ꜰᴀɴɴᴇᴅ herself briskly as she perused her dining table.

Mariah flirted coyly with Mr. Vanderworth whose stoic facade bore the faintest of smiles. Mildly satisfied, Gwynneth turned her attention to Miss Vanderworth, who appeared to be squinting less this evening, and was engaged in an animated conversation with Gladstone Pennington. She was happy to see the young man knew how to do the pretty. At the opposite end of the table, Sir Percy Allendale watched them all with keenest interest, while continuing to stuff himself with the quite delicious trifle the chef had prepared for dessert. The sad rattle was probably hoping for another tidbit of gossip to entice the bored ton.

Which was precisely why she had invited both young men to this intimate little dinner; it wouldn't hurt to keep an eye on the boy, making sure she was a step ahead of whatever game he chose to play. That was why she had gone on and on about the lovely letter, which existed solely in her imagination, of course, from Kathryn about the beauty of the Comte de Saville's ancestral estate and the elaborate plans to celebrate the upcoming wedding. Her fan slowed its pace—Gwynneth was actually quite pleased with how the evening was turning out.

"I don't care if she is at table!" a haughty female voice exclaimed from the foyer. An instant later the double doors flew open and a white-haired woman with beautiful translucent skin, which belied her years, pushed past a stunned Westley.

"Sybilla!" Gwynneth gasped, surging to her feet.

"Gwynneth," the Duchess of Culter acknowledged. Her shrewd eyes focused on Mariah who had risen and come to her godmother's side. "Kathryn, my dear child!" Sybilla gushed, rushing to embrace her.

"No, no, Sybilla. This is Mariah. *Not* Kathryn," Gwynneth insisted, noticing Sir Percy's enthralled expression and seeing absolute ruin facing them all.

"Of course it's Mariah," Sybilla stated flatly, stepping back. "She's too short for Jules anyway. Where is dear Kathryn?" she inquired, glancing down the table, her gaze only momentarily hesitating at Miss Vanderworth before going on.

"Your Grace, I thought the betrothal of long standing. How is it you don't know Lady Kathryn?" Sir Percy audaciously inquired.

Really what did Jacko see in the young rip, Gwynneth fumed, appalled at his lack of decorum.

Sybilla stood stock still, and lifted her delicate chin to stare down her extremely straight nose at Sir Percy. "Who are you?" she demanded.

Making a credible bow, he smiled. "Sir Percy Allendale, Your Grace. I am a friend of Lord Thistlewait."

"But how is this possible? Our friends have known anytime these last months about my darling Jules and Kathryn. It is only my ill health that has kept the formal announcement under wraps and me away from my future stepgrandaughter." Turning away, she cut him dead. "Obviously, sir, you are an imposter. Gwynneth, your servants should show this man the door." Sybilla commanded before reclining into Gwynneth's chair.

"But ... but ..." Percy sputtered, glancing around, a dazed expression glazing his eyes.

Gladstone had the good sense to take his friend's arm. "We'll be taking our leave now, Lady Tutwilliger. Thank you for a delicious dinner." With a hasty bow and one quick smile at Miss Vanderworth, he ushered a stricken Sir Percy away.

"My sister and I shall also take our leave, Lady Tutwilliger. You obviously have family matters to attend to. We also thank you for a lovely evening," Mr. Vanderworth said in his usual calm voice.

Really, did nothing *ever* rattle the man? Gwynneth wondered if she should reconsider her decision to encourage his attentions to Mariah. But that young lady obviously found no fault with his correct bow as he bid her good night. Westley appeared, playing the role of the perfect butler to a nicety, for once, to escort Mariah and the Vanderworths to the front door.

Only then did she notice the man standing at the other end of the table. How had he gotten past her eagle eye?

Every time Gwynneth laid eyes on the Marquis of Aubrey she wished she was thirty years younger. If Jacko's beautiful looks matured into this glorious specimen of mature male, she would be more than repaid for all the worry he had given her.

Dominic gave her one of his breathtaking smiles. "Lady Tutwilliger, I apologize for interrupting your dinner party." He flashed a rueful glance at the duchess. "Grandmother couldn't wait to see you."

"Of course I couldn't wait!" complained Sybilla. "How could I after that dreadful communication." She rounded on Gwynneth. "Where is Jules? What have you done to him?"

"Done to him! I found him in bed with my sweet Kathryn!" Gwynneth retaliated.

The battle was joined!

"Willy, whatever is going on here?" gasped Mariah, coming back into the dining room and quickly closing the doors behind her. "Your voices can be heard all over the house. It's bad enough without the servants gossiping."

"Lady Mariah, perhaps you can explain to us what has occurred," Dominic asked, coming to stand with his hand on the duchess's shoulder to calm her. "Grandmother, for once, let someone else get a full sentence in."

Mariah's wide, soft eyes asked her godmother for permission to tell the story. Gwynneth nodded with a sigh.

"Kathryn and Jacko are twins, you know," Mariah began, her fingers tightly gripped together before her. "Kat foolishly pursued him to the Blue Boar Inn to try to keep him from some mischief. She has always seen it as her duty to keep him out of trouble because she is the elder."

With a gentle smile, Dominic urged her on. "We understand. But how did my brother become a part of this?"

"She was waiting for Jacko in his room at the inn . . . and . . . and somehow . . . the comte mistook his room . . . and . . . and they were sharing a bed

66

. . . when we arrived," Mariah finished quickly, her cheeks two bright red spots.

"Obviously it was a mistake. If it was just family why could it not be kept quiet?" Dominic asked, a slight edge in his voice now.

"Because that dreadful rattle Sir Percy was with Jacko at the Blue Boar Inn. He saw all!" declared Gwynneth.

"Oh, my God, not that insufferable twit!" scoffed Sybilla. "Then they must wed at once! No, no, Dominic, there is no choice." Sybilla patted his hands that now tightly gripped her shoulders. "Where are they now?"

"On their way to Château Saville with Lord Thistlewait and my companion, Miss Hannah Hamilton, to chaperon them. But I know when they arrive Kat plans to cry off from the engagement!"

Gwynneth's admiration for Dominic was in jeopardy when she spied his relieved look. "However, we cannot allow that. Kat has already cried off from one engagement. Another would be doom for her expectations. I have a plan. But I'll need your support, Sybilla. We must confer."

"Grandmother, no!" Dominic protested as the duchess leaned forward, interested. "Jules deserves more than an arranged marriage. He deserves what I share with Juliana. After all the years . . . I have just found him—"

The duchess quieted him with a raised finger and a loving smile. "My dear boy, do you think I do not know what is owed your brother? I have an idea of my own that will insure we do not lose him again."

"Kathryn, are you feeling unwell?" Hannah leaned forward in the coach seat to take Kat's hand.

67

"Good. You don't feel overly warm, but you are un-characteristically pale."

Kat forced a smile. "No, I am fine, truly. Just a trifle fatigued from the journey."

Hannah sighed and reclined against the pillows. With a small yawn, she nodded. "I certainly understand, dear." Then she promptly closed her eyes.

Caroline was already napping, one cheek resting against the coach curtains. Kat couldn't sleep. All she could think about was this latest development. She hadn't slept a wink after her conversation with Jacko and Saville. Her worst fears had been confirmed: Sir Edmund Trigge was capable of anything. What could Kat do to protect them all from his wrath? She had come up with no solution during the long, sleepless night.

This morning she had tried to cover the bruising shadows under her eyes with a perky manner, but she must have failed for Jules had given her a most penetrating gaze when he handed her into the coach, and now Hannah had noticed. She would have to be very careful not to give herself away again. Her twin, usually attuned to her every mood, would cajole until he wrested the truth from her, and then the fat would be in the fire. She sensed a restlessness in him, a sudden yearning, that might easily be turned into a hollow, chivalrous gesture. She had no doubt how a duel between her brother and Edmund Trigge would turn out.

She turned to the young, sleeping girl beside her. Caroline's cheeks were lightly flushed just below where her lashes fanned. She looked very young and very helpless. Kat could not have done differently; she could not have stood by and allowed someone like Trigge to ruin this innocent's life. Now she must deal with the consequences.

Jules's reaction she was not quite so sure of . . . nor, the fate of any duel he might undertake. In a mere two days she had come to know him as a man of strength and honor and compassion. She owed him her good name, and Caroline's, and perhaps even Jacko's life. There was no way she could embroil him further, especially a little voice nagged inside her, because she intended to cry off.

Perhaps Trigge will just give up and leave us in peace, Kat's usual optimistic nature decreed. He couldn't possibly follow them to Saville's home. There they would all be safe. Perhaps, if Jules did not mind, she would take a trifle longer than first planned to end their engagement.

When would they arrive? She needed to beg Jules's indulgence until she could be sure they were safely away from Sir Edmund Trigge.

The gently rolling countryside was covered with grapevines as far as the eye could see. Occasionally Kat could spy a great household way back, up on a hill, or the coach would pass an elaborate gateway.

Finally, Jules signaled the coach to turn into a roadway that hadn't been dragged for years. The two other occupants of the coach were jolted awake by the vibration before, mercifully, they came to a halt.

Château Saville was enormous. Four stories of stone rose straight up to the sky. There were no towers or battlements and Kat, absurdly, wondered how the place had ever been defended.

Inexplicably, Jules was attuned to her thoughts. "I only remember a few of the stories I've been told about the house. Apparently it had been planned as a summer palace, but the knight was lost in the crusades. It stood empty until my great-great-grandfather was titled. He was really the one who finished the château and planted the vineyard."

Jules glanced around wonderingly. "I remember it as much larger."

Jacko assisted Caroline and Hannah from the coach. Jules walked across the crushed brown rock, at least here some attempt had been made to rake it level, and rang a bell hidden to one side of the *porte cochère*. At once the door was flung wide. A tall, painfully thin woman walked out. Her gray hair was pulled tightly back into a bun and she wore a stiff black dress corded round with an eye-catching set of gold keys.

"Mon dieu! Monsieur le Comte, you are the image of your late father!" she exclaimed and then gasped as Jules turned fully to face her and she saw his left cheek. Her eyes widened for an instant before she stopped herself. Taking a deep breath, she hurried down to meet them.

"I am Madelaine Bernair, the *ménagère* of Château Saville. You will not remember me, you were so young when you fled the terror." She crossed herself. "My parents were in charge then. Now I am housekeeper and my husband, Anton, estate manager. Our families have long served the *famille* Devereaux, and we preserved as much as we could during these long years."

"Madame Bernair," Jules bowed to her, taking one of her gnarled hands between his palms. "My solicitor has told me of your devotion to my home. It shall not be forgotten. Now I want you to meet my guests."

Once again he gave Kat a smile that caused the

oddest sensations in strange parts of her anatomy. This time he also took her hand, leading her forward. "My fiancée, Lady Kathryn Thistlewait. Her brother, Lord Thistlewait."

Kat noticed the usual stunned stare from Madame Bernair when she and Jacko stood side by side.

"Miss Hannah Hamilton and Miss Caroline Strange," he continued.

"Welcome to Château Saville," Madame Bernair replied coolly to the introductions, her dark gaze unapproachable. "I have made rooms ready and ordered a light repast that will be served in the dining hall in one hour."

Exhausted from her sleepless night, Kat brushed off her uneasiness at Madame Bernair's chilly greeting. Everything else seemed in order as they moved slowly through the house. The rooms were immaculate, if sadly out-of-date. Here and there, Kat could see bright patches on the walls where pictures should have hung. There was much to be done here. Perhaps she could repay Jules's kindness to them all by assisting in the redecoration of the house. Fresh hangings and a more comfortable arrangement of furniture could do a lot to make this seem more a home.

The carved four-poster bed in Kat's chamber was beautiful; the rich patina of the old wood making her run her fingers over its smoothness. Here, as in the other rooms she had seen, the brocade draperies were faded and she could see where the bedcovers and hangings had been carefully mended.

All along their journey they had seen the marks of war; in the countryside and in the people. The château also bore its scars.

Hurriedly pouring water in a porcelain bowl, Kat freshened herself. Just a few tugs on a hairbrush brought her unruly mop into order among the ribbons. She changed quickly from her traveling dress to a simple at-home muslin in a sea green she knew enhanced her natural coloring. Now she was ready to meet the others. She knew she was early, but she hoped she might find Jules in the small salon where they were to gather before supper. She wished a word in private to assess whether or not he would object if she and the others stayed on for a while.

It was clear the small salon was the one room in which Madame Bernair had placed the treasures she had been able to save. On the mantel an antique French clock ticked—it looked like pictures she'd seen. Vaguely she remembered there'd been a French king who'd delighted in making clocks— a Louis, she thought—and wondered if this could be one of his. On the tables were placed fawn leatherbound books, and at the windows the deep green brocade draperies still retained their rich color. But the most outstanding treasure was the huge oil painting over the fireplace.

She now knew exactly what Jules would be like without his patch and scar. The man staring down at her had expressive, large, dark eyes, heavily rimmed with lashes; the high cheekbones gave his face strength and character, as did the mouth, although it was curved in such an appealing smile that it exposed an underlying sweetness. It was not a beautiful face such as Jacko's, instead it mesmerized and compelled, making one wish to know what lurked behind that dark gaze and to experience the delights that smile promised.

The woman was breathtakingly beautiful, but her perfection of face and figure made her appear unreal. But not so the baby she held in her arms. Jules had probably been about a year old when this was done. His soft baby face was alight with joy and curiosity, his expressive eyes bright above his rosy chubby cheeks.

"It was done shortly before my father died."

Kat whirled around. He was standing in the open doorway, staring up at the painting.

With lightning clarity Kat realized the patch and scar made not a whit of difference; Jules himself, as he was, stirred within her all the emotions she had felt while studying the painting. She wanted to know him better. It was a slightly frightening realization.

Taking a calming breath to still her suddenly racing pulse, she smiled. "It is a wonderful painting. You were an adorable baby."

The unpatched brow lifted questioningly and the wonderful smile which, obviously, was a legacy from his father, curved his mouth. "I look as if I might have been a troublemaker."

"Yes, that, too." Kat laughed, glancing again at the painting. "Your mother was beautiful." Looking back, Kat's breath caught in her throat. Jules's smile had disappeared. In its place was such cold anguish that a chill shook her.

"Yes, she was," he said in a flat voice, before turning away. "Good evening, Miss Hamilton. Miss Strange ... Ah, Jacko, you are just in time. I believe our meal is ready."

The dining hall was just that, a large lofty room, its wall hung with priceless tapestries that, miraculously, Madame had saved during the terror and its aftermath of senseless plundering. One exceptional piece depicted classical gods lying about on a grassy meadow playing music to one another.

Jules was pleased with the supper. It seemed he had a staff to be grateful for. He remembered none of them, although Madame must have been in the house before he left. He did, however, remember the one tapestry and the large ring of keys the housekeeper carried. A difficult thing to deal with— his childhood memories. He smiled faintly. His guests had just finished the dessert soufflé and all looked content. Except Kathryn; he had sensed all evening that she wished to speak privately with him. That was easily enough arranged.

"I am afraid my cellar is not yet complete, Jacko," he apologized. "Shall we forgo our port and join the ladies for coffee?"

"Capital idea, Saville!" Jacko leapt to his feet. "Actually in the mood for cards. Are you game?"

"Oh, I'd love to play!" declared Caroline.

"You like cards, Miss Strange?" Jacko uttered with a shocked stare at her excited face.

"Oh, yes! My guardian, Sir George Bartholomew, was an inveterate player. He taught me everything he knew. I'm quite good," she declared proudly.

"We'll see about that." Jacko laughed, leading the way back to the small salon.

Miss Hamilton browsed through the leather-bound volumes, found one in English and seated herself quietly in a corner. Jules very kindly took an extra candelabrum to her chair. Kathryn's imploring glance evoked an alarming eagerness to discover what was bothering her.

Jacko and Caroline, each possessing a quite brilliant glint in his or her eye, already had seated themselves at a table.

"Would you mind playing piquet? I wish Lady Kathryn's opinion of the gardens," he drawled.

Jacko didn't even glance up. Obviously his brotherly urge to chaperon was not as strong as his gamemanship. "You go ahead. Miss Strange and I shall amuse ourselves."

"Oh, yes, Lord Thistlewait," Caroline said with great confidence, turning up a card. "I believe it is my deal."

"Thank you, my lord. I need to speak with you about a matter of great urgency," Kathryn whispered as he led her through a doorway onto a small flagstone terrace circled round by a charming flower garden.

"I sensed you wished to speak alone. Besides, I truly would like your opinion of the landscape," he offered, knowing she might like a few moments of grace before she talked about whatever it was she dreaded so. It was strange how easily he had come to understand her moods.

She strolled from flower bed to flower bed, occasionally stopping to lift a heavy bloom to her face.

"I would say your gardener is doing an excellent job. These are quite lovely." She straightened, turning to gaze up at him. "Jules, I've been thinking about my plan to cry off. If you don't mind, I believe we should change it."

He felt as if a fist had slammed into his chest. Never had he intended to allow her to cry off, but he hadn't dreamed she would come to that decision on her own. He moved a step closer, his pulse doing an odd uneven beat. "Lady Kathryn—"

"Never fear I plan to hold you to this ridiculous engagement," she interrupted hastily.

Even in the moonlight he could see how her skin flushed with color. His own felt much the same, suddenly scorched and sensitive.

"It is just that I owe you a great debt and . . . and I wish to repay it." Lifting her chin, she met his gaze steadily. "You have been quite wonderfully kind to go along with my scheme so I would like to repay you by assisting you in the restoration of the château. Willy says I'm quite good at household management. And besides, to cry off so soon after we have become engaged would be too ramshackle. Well, Jules, what do you think?" she finished in a much smaller voice than she had began.

A perfect excuse to give him more time to woo Kathryn he could not have thought up himself, although he disliked the thought that she felt indebted to him. "If that is your wish, then it is mine," he said softly, smiling.

To his surprise, her eyes widened and a pulse began to throb in her throat. She placed her fingers over her smooth skin.

"Thank you, Jules. You are so very kind. I—"

"Oh, Kathryn, I beat him!" Caroline crowed, bursting out onto the terrace.

"Girl's a regular card shark," Jacko grumbled from the doorway. "Not myself tonight. Tomorrow we'll have a rematch."

Caroline clapped her hands, giving Kathryn a quick hug. "Your brother is a poor loser," she laughed. "Oh, my yes, Lord Thistlewait, I'll be delighted to beat you again tomorrow."

"I . . . I believe we should all retire now. None of us are quite ourselves tonight," Kathryn said softly, no doubt attempting to head off the retort all could see forming on her brother's face.

Jules remained on the terrace after they left him, laughing together, eagerly making plans for the morrow. He had never fully understood his reason for giving in to Lady Tutwilliger's demand for an engagement or for agreeing to Kathryn's plan, although he had always intended to make her see reason.

Now he felt adrift. Kathryn, Jacko, Caroline, even Hannah in her quiet way, had helped to make this homecoming easier. He'd been so concerned about all of them he hadn't had a chance to dwell on the unpleasant memories. He'd cut himself off from normal society far too long. Like Dominic, he had allowed the incident at Culter Towers to dominate his life. Look at the happiness Dominic had finally found! For an instant, when Kathryn had said she wasn't going to end their engagement, he had felt that kind of joy. Then she had gone on with her reasoning and the joy had fled, leaving only a determination. . . . He was a man who had always been sure of himself and honest about his own actions. Yet, in his dealings with Kathryn he seemed to be acting upon impulse instead of logic.

"Monsieur le Comte," Madame Bernair broke into his thoughts and he turned to her. She stood before him holding a cream vellum envelope.

"This arrived by messenger before dinner. I did not wish to disturb you with your guests."

Strolling back into the salon he broke the seal. Quickly reading, he stopped Madame Bernair before she retired. "Madame, were you aware that Monsieur Castlemagne was in residence?"

"Non, monsieur," she shook her head.

"Then you had not informed any of his servants that I was due with a house party?"

"Non, monsieur," she repeated.

"That will be all," he said absently, staring into the ashes of the fireplace. An old name Castlemagne—one of his father's friends. It was amazing he was still alive. Jules would be delighted to call on him. In a small community it was probably impossible to keep any secrets, still Jules wondered how Castlemagne had known that he had returned.

Chapter 7

THE FOUR-POSTER BED was quite comfortable; the linens, although mended, smelled of sunshine and a hint of lilacs; the pillows were plump and the mattress was firm beneath her. There was no explanation for why she couldn't sleep. She was exhausted from the trip. Not the travel itself, but the circumstances surrounding it. Unfamiliar feelings and questions bound up in her relationship to Jules, her championship of Caroline, but most of all, her fear of Edmund Trigge. She'd never had to fear before. Her body was nearly numb with fatigue as she lay curled on the bed, but her mind careened forward—filled with pictures, very attractive pictures of Jules. Jules at ease, sprawled in the taproom of the Blue Boar Inn; bemused, his shirt open, struggling to deal with the onslaught of her entire family; alert, exuding power and confidence as he faced down Sir Edmund; and amused, struggling to hide his smile each time Hannah conveniently took one of her little naps. He had, nearly from the moment of their meeting, shown her nothing but kindness. She could not help but wonder what was behind his courtesy to her.

Was she like Caroline, vulgarly curious about him? How little she knew of his emotions. His thoughts were a mystery to her. Kat did not think his air of detachment assumed, it was simply a part of him. Tonight, in the salon, she had fully realized his appeal, which more than ever made her wish to understand him. Somehow she knew that meant getting him to trust her enough to reveal how he had received his wound.

Sighing, Kat turned over, seeking a cool space on the pillow to rest her hot cheek. Finally she closed her eyes, willing herself to stop thinking of Jules. Ever so slowly she felt her mind let go and begin to drift away, but just before she slept she realized the visions of Jules had pushed all dread of Sir Edmund away.

Noir, eager for a gallop, pulled at the reins until Jules gave him his head. The early morning mist swirled before them, hiding everything ahead on the road. Not until he reached the hillcrest did Jules pull the horse to a stop. Noir pawed the earth, snorting, impatient to be off, but Jules stilled him as he gazed down at his home.

The château was, compared to Culter Towers, a modest house. But, surrounded by terraced vineyards stretching up the sides of the lush green valley it presented a certain appeal. Generations of Savilles had thrived here, allied to the French king, until the great revolution shattered their world. Strange, Jules thought, none of those Saville ghosts called to him. He felt no bond to this place; how could it feel like home? England—Culter Towers— had been home since he was five years old, and it held the only family he had left, the only people he loved.

Noir reared slightly and Jules reined him in before beginning, slowly, to make his way down into the next valley. It was too early for a morning call, Jules knew, for he had left all his guests still abed, even Jacko. But he could not wait to discover how his father's old friend, Gustave Castlemagne, had known he was here.

A niggling uneasiness had kept him tossing and turning all night. He refused to dwell on what, or should he confess who else had disturbed his slumber.

Château Castlemagne was in much better condition than his own home, and when the butler showed him into a small sitting room, Jules immediately saw it had been freshly painted and refurbished. The healing of the wounds was good to see.

"Monsieur le Comte, the master is still abed," the butler began. "I—"

Jules held up his palm. "Do not disturb him. I shall leave my card. Please give him my regrets that my houseguests and I shall not be in residence long. Perhaps some afternoon that is convenient we could talk over the old days. I'd like to hear some stories of my father." Jules continued, as if compelled to ask. "I am surprised that Monsieur Castlemagne knew I had returned."

"He was delighted to learn you had come from England with our houseguest, Sir Edmund Trigge."

Jules forced a smile. "I see. Is Sir Edmund about?"

"I believe he has gone for a morning ride, Monsieur le Comte."

"Thank you," Jules murmured thoughtfully. What new mischief could Trigge be up to? Outside he took the reins from the groom and vaulted into the saddle. Obviously, Noir sensed his distraction. He pawed impatiently and quivered with excitement. "Not this time, my friend." Jules whispered, leaning over to stroke the horse's silky mane. "This time we do not race. We hunt."

Luck was with him. Less than a mile from the château Sir Edmund crossed his path. Jules blocked the center of the road, Noir prancing delicately. Edmund had little choice but to bring his horse to a standstill, for the roadside was lined with a thick hedge which allowed for no escape.

"Alone this time, Saville?" He sneered, his beady eyes flicking about nervously. "No young pup of the ton to aid you?"

"I need no help where you are concerned, Trigge," Jules spit out, lunging forward to grip Edmund's reins. "I'm sure you recall the last time we disagreed on the subject of a young lady." Edmund's face flushed scarlet as Jules continued, "I've warned you once already, and you did not heed me."

"Let go of my reins!" Sir Edmund sputtered, "Or answer the consequences!"

Jules laughed harshly. "Your memory is failing you, Trigge. I believe you challenged me to a duel once before and I refused. A duel of honor can only be conducted between equals. And you are certainly not my equal! I feel it would be better for your health if you were to quit this part of France, *immediatement!*"

"You go too far, Saville," he hissed, tugging frantically at the reins Jules still held in an iron grip.

"It is you who go too far. Stay away from those I call my friends, Trigge, or you shall be sorry. Since you are no gentleman, honor will not constrain me." Disgusted, Jules tossed the reins at Edmund. "Definitely cut short your visit with Gustave. Your presence in Champagne is an offense."

Jules danced Noir back and the horse reared in eagerness, making Sir Edmund's steed suddenly bolt and tumble him to the dusty roadway.

Jules didn't bother to laugh as the horse galloped, reins flapping, toward Castlemagne. Instead, he directed Noir delicately around the vanquished rider, sprawled inelegantly in the dirt.

Edmund sat up and shook his fist. "You'll answer for this, Saville! All of you will!"

Paying no heed, Jules gave his horse his head and they cantered home.

Madame Bernair's deliberately cool air had not risen one degree all morning long. Dutifully, she showed Kat the linen closets, the pantries, and the small store of silver, crystal, and china that had been saved from the terror. Even Caroline's exuberance and eagerness to learn when she joined them halfway through the inspection did not change Madame's sour expression in the slightest. The only shift on her placid face occurred when Jacko found them in the library. Then some emotion flirted through her eyes as she gazed between them.

"We are twins, Madame Bernair," Kat quietly informed her.

"I see that," she stated flatly, before turning to the cabinet and continuing. "These are only a few of the original books that escaped the plunder." She opened one glass-fronted door. "Here is a small dress sword we found after the looting. And these inlaid dueling pistols were hidden by my parents."

"By gad, they're beauties!" Jacko breathed, picking one pistol up, its mother of pearl and gold handle reflecting the light from the windows. He tested its weight on his palm. "Feels perfectly balanced. Love to try their aim." He slid Kat a dimpled smile. "Saville won't mind. My future brother-in-law after all. Percy and Glady say all I need is more practice to be a credible shot."

Kat doubted if all the practice in the world would help Jacko's aim, but the diversion might keep her mind off Jules. Where could he be this morning? He had not appeared at breakfast, and they had not encountered him all morning during their tour of the château.

After thanking Madame for the tour, Kat gratefully excused herself. She had a better feel for the household and some definite ideas on how to improve its management, but she was hesitant to approach Madame at her most formidable.

Later that afternoon she was no closer to solving her problem. Madame still wore a slightly disapproving air. Her husband, Anton, was a different story. He had been all that was amiable. He suggested they shoot by an abandoned storage shed and had set up several targets.

Caroline laughingly demurred when offered a pistol. For some twenty minutes Jacko had been firing before he finally nicked a target.

Caroline diplomatically refused to comment, but Kat kept encouraging him.

"No, no. Don't jerk so. Squeeze the trigger ... like this." She brought the pistol level, aimed, and fired. As always, she hit the bull's-eye.

"Oh, Kathryn, that is truly remarkable!" Caroline clapped her hands.

"Blasted unfair if you ask me," Jacko grumbled. "My sister's a better shot. Embarrassing."

"Oh, my lord, you are a superb horseman. That is much better than being a crack shot. So much more useful," Caroline soothed, and to Kat's surprise Jacko's sulky face brightened in a dimpled smile.

Suddenly Kat felt Jules's presence. Out of the corner of her eye she could just see him, one shoulder leaning against a tree, his legs braced apart as he watched them.

Turning slowly, she faced him and smiled welcomingly. "Good afternoon. We missed you this morning."

Jules strolled toward them. "Yes, I understand you had a tour of the château. I hope you are not so tired after your target practice that a ride through the vineyards would be too taxing. I believe you will find it quite picturesque, Lady Kathryn."

"Oh, Comte, did you see Kathryn's shot?" Caroline eagerly inquired.

His dark penetrating gaze rested on her face, and Kat suddenly found the sunlight too bright and the warmth of the day a trifle overpowering.

"Yes, it was very impressive. I must add this to the list of Lady Kathryn's many accomplishments," he praised, his face transformed by a warm smile. "Miss Strange, you and Jacko are welcome to join us for the ride," he added lazily.

"Oh, thank you, Comte, but unfortunately I am not a good horsewoman. Lord Thistlewait is welcome to join you." Caroline's little face tensed, awaiting Jacko's reply.

"Saville, think I'll stay and keep Miss Strange

company," he offered, a slight redness coloring him to his earlobes.

Kat hid her surprise and amusement but was nearly undone at the radiant smile with which Caroline rewarded him. Sisterly feelings indeed!

"Oh, Lord Thistlewait, we could play piquet! I believe you challenged me to another game, did you not?"

Really the girl knew exactly how to deal with her twin. They all turned for the château but Jules caught her arm and whispered conspiratorially, "It seems it will be just the two of us, Lady Kathryn."

A frisson of pleasure flickered through her.

The idea of riding alone with Jules made her all thumbs while she changed into her dark blue riding habit. The maids were all busy elsewhere and Kat didn't like to take them from their duties when she was perfectly capable of dressing herself.

Peering into the mirror, she was quite pleased with the results. For once she had even gotten the tilt of the riding hat just right so the white ostrich plume brushed her cheek.

Jules was waiting for her on the front steps. Grooms held Noir, only a little less frisky than before, and a beautiful chestnut stallion whose name, Jules informed her, was Café au Lait.

Jules frowned, peering up into a sky of huge gray clouds. "Perhaps we should postpone our ride."

"How unfortunate. I was so looking forward to it," Kat sighed deeply.

Jules shot her a sharp look. "Then we shall not disappoint you. Let us attempt it." With a nod from him, the grooms brought the horses forward, and Jules tossed her into the saddle.

The air felt cooler as they cantered away from

the château. There was a definite feel of a storm brewing, but Kat ignored it. She had decided that for her own peace of mind she wished to get to know Jules better. What better way than to spend some time alone with him.

With alarming regularity, Kat was finding Jules's perception of her taste correct. The ride was beautiful, soothing. Her concerns were easily left behind. They cantered away from the gardens and orchard, near where the targets had been set up. At a slight rise Jules slowed and pointed to landmarks below them.

"Somewhere in the vineyards above us, near a hidden cave, is the winery. In my father's journals he states our wine was superior because it aged in that natural coolness." He laughed, a free clear peal that echoed around them. "Perhaps I can make his dream come true."

"Dream?" Kat questioned.

"Let me show you."

They turned down a rutted track. Grapevines curled around posts, reaching strong tentacles to support their heavy load of fruit. The sun had disappeared behind rolling gray clouds, cooling the air; a fresh light breeze tickled the plume against her cheek. The breeze also ruffled Jules's thick black hair so it fell forward, but as always he smoothed it back with his long, thin fingers.

They entered a small clearing with a huge wooden wagon filled with grapes. Bowing deeply, one of the vineyard workers presented her with a cluster of grapes on an earthenware plate. They were newly washed, drops of water still clinging to them as Kat nibbled. They were delicious, sweet and moist.

"Jules, they are wonderful! Here, you must try." Impulsively, she held out a grape and he took it from her hand and tasted.

He gave the eager worker his most charming smile. "Excellent. My compliments. Now, Lady Kathryn, we must try to outrace the storm back to the château."

She laughed as he tossed her up into the saddle. "Your land is beautiful. I'm so glad I had this opportunity to see it."

"Yes, the land is recovering. Now if I can only return you safely to the château without you getting a thorough soaking."

They let the horses go but were hardly beyond the vineyard to a wooded area when the crack of a pistol stopped them abruptly.

Three shouting, masked men surged out of the woods on horseback.

"Kathryn, turn!" Jules commanded and she wheeled her horse around, but was stopped by another brigand whose black mask covered his eyes. The lower half of his face was obscured by a strategically tied neckerchief.

Noir wheeled and danced beneath Jules and he brought him sharply under control to come to Kat's side. "Don't be frightened," he whispered. Although her heart pounded so strongly she felt it in every cell of her body she nodded.

Three of the masked men dropped to the ground and tried to grab Noir's reins, but the black stallion reared, and they fell back before him.

"If you wish money we have none with us," Jules stated coolly. "If you are wise men you will give this up and leave my land."

The man behind Kat shouted in response to

Jules's careful statement. His was not the polite schoolroom French that Kat knew, and she had great difficulty trying to understand. All she clearly picked out was that these ruffians knew who Jules was. Suddenly she felt something cold and sharp pressing into her temple. The man holding her, the ringleader, obviously threatened her.

Jules again flickered that reassuring smile that said: "It's all right, I'm here, trust me." She realized in that instant she did trust him, completely.

To Kat's horror the instant Jules dismounted, one of the ragged looking men lifted his pistol and struck him near his eye.

She screamed as he crumbled to the ground, all fear for her personal safety receding before her desperate need to reach him. Disregarding everything, she flung herself off the horse, but before she had taken two steps strong burly arms caught her.

"Non, Mademoiselle . . ." was all she understood, but the brute laughed, pulling her arms painfully behind her.

As she watched in mounting horror, Jules was lifted to his feet and held between two of the men while the third kicked him in the stomach before punching him again and again on the face.

Kat had to get to him! She had been kicking and thrashing desperately at her captor; in response he had only tightened his arms around her. He reeked of whiskey and Kat could only hope he was slightly foxed or her plan wouldn't work. She suddenly went limp, sinking nearly to her knees, and as she hoped, he loosened his grip. At that instant she elbowed him sharply in the groin. With a bellow he doubled over in pain and Kat grabbed his pistol that had fallen in the dust. Twirling, she snatched another from the horse holster.

The three men were so engrossed in attacking Jules they didn't notice her until she screamed, *"Arrêtez!"*

Mouths gaping open, they all turned to her. The burly one who had been striking Jules sneered at her, a vulgar epithet she was sure.

In answer she lifted one pistol, aimed and shot his hat off. "The second shot will kill one of you," she promised grimly in English. The tone of her voice more than her words must have convinced the ruffian.

He backed up. His two companions were so stunned they dropped Jules, and he fell to his knees. Suddenly he rolled sideways to launch himself up to land a bruising punch to one of his assailant's jaws.

"Kathryn, bring the gun to me," he gasped, swaying on his feet.

Before she could think or move they were gone, even her captor, who still doubled over, limped to his horse and scrambled upon it.

Kat let them go, nothing mattered but reaching Jules.

Blood from a cut above his eyes pooled around his patch before dripping down his cheek to his bruised jaw.

Dropping the pistols, she gathered him in her arms, trying to steady him. "Jules, are you all right?" she cried.

Something sharp, piercing, and sweet engulfed her heart as he tried to smile.

"I believe, Kathryn, I must sit down."

A sudden clap of thunder made them both glance up.

"Not here, Jules," she said matter-of-factly, although she was beside herself with concern for him. "The storm is breaking. The trees will offer some protection."

And they did. The heavy branches meeting overhead created a canopy of leaves so they were spared much of the drenching from the sudden downpour.

Jules sank against a tree, his face totally without color save for where the blood marked it.

"The winery," he gasped, "just ahead. We can shelter there."

She braced him carefully and muttering words of encouragement, half led, half dragged him to the low-ceilinged building.

"I believe my ribs are broken." Jules finally managed to say, disbelief plain on his battered face.

She pried the door open, its heavy hinges squeaking from disuse. The interior was dusty, but even so the perfume of grape hung in the air. Not unpleasant, she thought inconsequentially. The room was dominated by the great circular wooden press; barrels filled a far wall. There were only a few benches—no place comfortable for Jules, so she eased him to the floor.

"Did they hurt you, Kathryn?" he asked sharply, scanning her face.

"No. I sincerely hope I hurt *them* more than they did me. But it is you who needs attention," she said briskly, and began to unbutton her jacket. Removing it, she tugged her lawn shirt free and cavalierly ripped a large strip from the bottom, exposing her chemise underneath.

"Kathryn, what are you doing?" He lifted that

91

haughty brow but the affect was nullified by his grimace of pain. "I believe your being semiclothed is how this all began," he chuckled, a little breathlessly. "Do you think this is a good idea?"

"I think it is an excellent idea to see to your wounds. According to Willy all the damage to my reputation has been done already."

She marched to the doorway and stuck the remnants of her lawn shirt out into the downpour until it was soaked.

Wringing it out somewhat, she carried it back and fell on her knees beside Jules.

He tried to struggle up. "Kathryn, you don't—"

She placed her hand on his shoulder, urging him to relax. "Do be quiet, my lord." She fussed with assumed agitation. "Just let me do what must be done."

He stayed perfectly motionless beneath her hands as she bathed the cut above his eye and the streaks of dried blood down his lean cheek. But when she moved toward the crusty black pool at his patch, iron fingers stilled her hand.

"No!" he whispered harshly.

"I must," she pleaded. "There might be a cut underneath, there is so much blood there. It will become infected if not cleansed."

Staring into his tense face all the piercing sweet sharpness that had engulfed her heart consumed her. Blinking back tears she widened her eyes. "You know this does not matter to me. Please. Please let me help you," she begged, unable to keep one short sob from her voice.

"It's not a pretty sight." He protested once more. Then with a harsh intake of breath, he nodded.

Gently, she lifted the patch and sensed him literally cease breathing.

Carefully, she bathed away the encrusted blood and was relieved to see there was no new cut near his scar.

Kat had spoken the truth; his sightless eye held no horror for her, rather she had a nearly overwhelming desire to press her lips there at the scar to soothe away his pain.

With trembling fingers she slid the patch back into place and their gazes entangled. She could see Jules begin to breathe again, then a flame, sudden and bright, flared in the depth of his eye.

Mesmerized, Kat had never wanted anything more than to cup his cheeks in her palms and touch that firm, expressive mouth with her own. Instead she turned away and began to rip long strips from her petticoat that she could use to wind around his chest.

Chapter 8

"SAVILLE! KAT! WHERE are you? Saville!"

Jacko's voice rang out sharply, breaking the spell that found her leaning so sweetly into Jules. How long they had been in the winery neither Jules or Kat could have guessed. At some time while she was wrapping his chest, his hands had risen to grip her shoulders. Both had been powerless against this force drawing them closer, their eyes locked, but now they each gave a breathless laugh, and his hands fell away.

Reluctantly, she rose to her feet. "It is Jacko searching for us. Stay here and I'll bring help."

She didn't realize until Jacko discovered them that he had disobeyed her and was standing, swaying with weakness, behind her. In one quick stride, Jacko was there to throw a supporting arm around Jules. "Saville, what happened? When the horses returned to the stables we knew something had gone awry.

"It was highwaymen, Jacko. But never mind that! Jules has been hurt. We must get him home soonest."

Jules straightened and she could see on his face the effort he made. "Your sister has been exceptionally brave, Jacko."

"Kat's always been a trooper," he remarked off-handedly, and pulled out a pistol, shooting into the air. "That's the signal. The others will come now."

Anton Bernair drove a cart into the clearing; others appeared on foot from the woods and the vineyard. Without help, Jules walked to the cart and hesitated only slightly before climbing up. The jolting was almost unbearable, but he never could have ridden a horse at this point. Kat watched him try to act blasé about the attack, downplaying the concern that all the searchers showed him. The cut above his patch began to bleed again. Jules flicked the drops away carelessly with his fingers. It took every ounce of willpower she possessed not to reach out and offer help, but some newly born instinct within her warned her away.

A nervously pacing Madame Bernair, flanked by Caroline and Hannah, waited for them at the front of the château.

"Oh, Kathryn, are you all right?" Caroline cried, rushing to Kat as a groom helped her down from the cart.

"I'm unhurt, Caroline." Kat reassured the young, frightened girl with a quick hug.

"I knew you would be fine, Kathryn," Hannah complimented as she slowly descended the steps. "I told them you were always remarkably resourceful."

In the few moments Hannah and Caroline had distracted her, Jules had attempted to get off the cart; instead he slid to the ground. The cut above his eye was now bleeding profusely.

Madame Bernair took her own crisp, white handkerchief and pressed it to his wound. For the first time Kat saw something besides cool dislike on Madame Bernair's face.

"Get a door to carry the comte to his chambers," she ordered a groom. "We'll have to send for a doctor."

"Thank you all, but I can manage on my own." Jules made another attempt to stand and, holding himself ramrod straight, his tone so commanding they all stepped back, haltingly walked toward the château. "It won't be necessary to take to my bedchamber."

Kat was not deterred by his imperious tone. She quickly took one arm, supporting him. Feeling it grow rigid beneath her fingers, she pleaded, "Jules, please let us go to our chambers for I am utterly exhausted from our adventure."

He flicked her a rueful glance, but nonetheless obeyed, entering the château and, slowly, they ascended the stairs to the second floor together.

His rooms were in the same hall as her own, only three doors away, so she allowed him to pass his chamber and deposit her at her own.

"Do you always get everyone to do your bidding so easily, Kathryn?" Jules asked quietly, amusement lurking in his voice.

"Is that a polite way of saying I am shockingly bossy, Monsieur le Comte?" she teased, resisting the urge to run soothing fingers over the bruises now beginning to discolor his lean cheeks.

"No." Gently, he lifted both her hands, and turning them palm up, pressed his lips to each in turn.

The trembling inside her threatened to overwhelm her, but she stilled it, staring up into his face.

"I am saying, my dear Kathryn, that you are the bravest woman I have ever known."

Again, a flame lit his gaze. But he stepped back, slowly releasing her hands. She put them behind her so he couldn't see their trembling. Knowing he would not go to his chamber, which he so obviously needed to do, until she did, Kat nodded and quickly entered her room, shutting the door quietly.

She leaned against it, listening, until she heard his footsteps fade down the hall. Only then could she drop upon her bed and bury her hot, tear-washed face in the pillows. She was instantly asleep, missing Hannah's peek into her room.

When Hannah returned hours later, bearing a tray with a bowl of strengthening broth, Kat consumed every bite. Hannah stood watching over her, arms folded with serene determination. "What an uproar this house has been in. The doctor, a very superior little man in a dark frock coat, has been to strap up the count and says he'll be fine—no bones broken, just deep bruises."

Hannah bustled about, insisting Kat change into her night shift and let her hair down. Kat knew Hannah was right; she should rest even though she longed to see for herself that Jules was all right. But after Hannah left, she lay wide awake and stared up at the underside of the floral canopy. She tossed and turned, making a jumble of the bedclothes.

There was only one way to make absolutely sure all was well. Slipping on her robe, Kat lifted a single candle and made her way out into the hall. She knocked softly on Jules's door, and when there was no reply, took a deep breath for courage, and entered his chamber.

He lay on his side, the cut above his left eye neatly bandaged. He was deeply asleep; his bare chest, wrapped tightly with linen strips, rose and fell slowly with strong, even breaths.

Weak with relief, she sat suddenly onto the side

of the bed, staring down at this man who had so completely complicated her life. Awake, he seemed so competent, so compelling. His air of authority had certainly scared off Edmund Trigge.

Kat knew Hannah trusted him utterly because she had so quickly settled into her old pattern here in France. Jacko thought him a great gun!

Even his staff, who hadn't known what kind of a master he would be, held him in affection. But now, asleep, he seemed vulnerable. His dark hair tumbled over his forehead, screening both the cut and the bruise that formed there. She reached out to brush it back as she had seen him do so many times.

"Lady Kathryn!" Madame Bernair gasped, and Kat stood to face the door.

Carrying a branched candelabrum, Madame Bernair quietly shut the door and came to stand beside her. "I slipped some laudanum into the tea I gave him for a light supper." At Kat's shocked look, Madame Bernair shrugged. "Men when they are unwell are like infants. It is our duty to see they do what is best for them."

"You have done an excellent job of caring for him. Thank you," Kat whispered, amazed that here in the dark and silence of Jules's room Madame was finally approachable. Without her sour expression her face was even softly pretty.

"I have had much practice. After the dreadful French defeat at Waterloo . . ." She crossed herself. "I nursed my son until, finally, his terrible wounds took his life."

"I am sorry, Madame." Kat saw such pain in the older woman's face, she felt tears welling up behind her own eyes. "The war took many fine young men."

"*Oui*, but it is hard at times." Madame Bernair

lifted her chin, assuming her natural pose, but with no dislike marring her countenance. "I will leave you alone with him. I know how important it is at these times to be with the one you love."

Kat was so stunned by Madame's words that she didn't even notice her departure. Love? She had always, from the time she was a child, sworn she would have a love as strong as her parents. A love, if need be, that could defy convention and flourish amid censure. But what would such a love feel like? She was certain it would not be like the love she felt for Jacko and Mariah. Love consumed you with its power. Like the piercing sharp sweetness that had consumed her earlier.

She now knew how foolish she had always been; you cannot seek love, you cannot consciously decide to love. Instead love finds you and pierces your heart before you even realize what's happening.

Running her fingertips ever so gently over Jules's bandaged cut and down the bruises discoloring his sleep-flushed cheeks, she acknowledged the truth. Through her foolhardy actions at the Blue Boar Inn she had stumbled into what she had always wanted. But how could Jules, forced into this coil by her foolishness, ever feel for her what now burned brightly in her heart?

Two days later, Jules insisted he was back to normal and came downstairs. The bruises were fading and the cut above his left eyebrow was healing. However, he noted that the women of the house still had a tendency to hover anxiously around him.

Most particularly he had sensed something new in Kathryn's attitude toward him. He wasn't sure what it meant.

It was not disgust after seeing his blind eye. He dared to hope it was the feelings that had been born between them in those moments in the winery. More and more he was growing certain that this arrangement they had fallen into would suit him very well indeed.

He retreated to his library to get away from Hannah's incessant flutterings. Concentrating on the *ménagère*'s books, he experienced no warning before the double doors burst open and Dominic casually strolled into the room.

"Dominic, *mon frère*! What are you doing here?" Joy at seeing his half brother warred with concern as to why he had dragged himself away from Juliana and the baby.

Dominic clapped him on the back, and although he smiled, his cornflower blue eyes were clouded. "I have come with two trunks of new frocks for Lady Kathryn, an English curate, and a special license. I have come to wish you happy," he drawled.

Shocked, Jules stepped away. "You know? But how? Lady Tutwilliger has already announced our engagement in the *Gazette*?"

"She and Grandmother have sent an announcement of your wedding, which *will* take place tomorrow. That's why I'm here." Dominic's startled eyes scanned his face. "Good God, I've just taken a good look at you! What has happened?"

"While out riding Kathryn and I were attacked by hired thugs. Fortunately, she was unharmed, they were set on getting me." Jules leaned lazily against the desk, his arms folded across his chest. He knew his brother well; he didn't want him to get involved.

100

"Hired! Hired by whom?" Dominic demanded, his face flushed with color.

"Easy, Dom. It is an old nemesis of mine, Sir Edmund Trigge. He was staying nearby, but has now suddenly disappeared."

"I know Trigge! Regular bounder! Still seen here and there at huge crushes, but definitely on the fringe. Do you wish me to deal with him when I return home?" Dominic asked grimly.

Dominic was older and less hot-headed than Kat's twin, but still there was a streak of daring easily recognized in his younger brother. In no way would he involve Dominic in this fight.

"Trigge I shall handle in time. Never fear. But more importantly, how are we to prepare Kathryn for her wedding day?" Jules smiled ruefully, but in all truth he felt his pulses quicken. He had made up his mind that day at the Blue Boar Inn to marry Kathryn Thistlewait. But then he had not really known her. Now that he did—"

"Jules . . . Jules, are you listening to me? Is there no other way? I . . . I wished you the kind of marriage I have with Juliana."

There was such concern and compassion in Dominic's eyes, Jules clasped his brother's arm. "*Mon frère*, I want this marriage. I am beginning to think Kathryn is as much my destiny as Juliana is yours."

Dominic's face softened as he lowered himself into a deep wing chair. Jules rang for a servant to ask Kathryn to attend him in the library, anxious for his brother to meet his future wife. As soon as Dom saw Kat he would be reassured of his happiness.

Moments later, Kat rushed in, her golden curls tumbling from lilac ribbons that barely held the richness of her hair, and her cheeks were flushed with fresh color. "Jules, are you all right? I'm sorry it took me so long, but I was on the third floor helping Madame Bernair air out bed hangings."

Dominic had risen upon her entrance, now she turned to acknowledge him. "I am sorry, I did not realize you had a guest."

"Kathryn, I would like you to meet my half brother, Dominic Crawford, Marquis of Aubrey. He has brought news from home."

Dominic performed a neat bow and gave her the smile that before his marriage, had littered the English countryside with broken hearts. "Lady Kathryn, I have brought letters and gifts from Lady Tutwilliger and your sister." He handed her two fat white envelopes. "I believe you should read the letters at once," he ordered, in a sharper than usual tone.

Frowning, Kat looked to Jules and he nodded. "It would be best if you read them now, Kathryn."

Although a puzzled crease marred her smooth brow, she sat on a needlepoint chair and slit open the envelope from Lady Tutwilliger.

Jules watched the varied emotions chase one another across her face as she read. She flushed, then she paled, then flushed again. Finally, she raised strickened aquamarine eyes to his face. It was the same imploring look she had given him before.

"Tomorrow?" she whispered.

"Yes," Dominic answered, his whole stance sterner than was his nature. "I have brought two trunks of bride clothes. I believe they are waiting in your chambers."

Jules silently signaled Dominic to leave the library. Waiting until the door closed tightly he knelt before her, taking both her cool hands between his palms. They were so close he could see tears welling beneath her long silky lashes and her full lower lip trembled ever so slightly. "I know you never intended to marry me. I am sorry your plan could not suffice, but I promise to do all in my power to make you not regret this marriage."

"I would ask but one question." She smiled faintly and, bemused, he leaned closer for she spoke in such soft tones he could barely hear her. "Does our marriage stop you from going where your heart goes?"

Their gazes locked and intertwined. "My answer is as your own, Kathryn," he answered quietly, although his heart, again, pumped in that odd, unsteady beat.

At her nod, he helped her to rise. She thrust up her chin, her eyes remarkably blue and clear. "Then tomorrow is our wedding day, Monsieur le Comte."

The wedding day dawned bright and clear. Kat saw the sun's first rays touch the hilltops and slowly, brilliantly, expand to bathe the valley in a golden glow. She had lain awake all night, reading and rereading Mariah's letter. Yet her attention had not been on the words so much as on the coming day. What would this marriage bring? Ideally she hoped that she and Jules would grow ever closer, sharing their thoughts and hopes.

At dinner Dominic had spoken so openly of his own marriage, his happiness was apparent to all. And when he had mentioned his baby son . . . Kat had looked across the table to find Jules watching her intently. The same thoughts whirled through her mind. Did Jules intend to make theirs a real marriage? Would he come to her tonight and consummate this union that had been thrust upon them? The thought did not frighten her as it would have a week ago. Jules was no longer a stranger to her. Yes, his thoughts and his emotions were still a mystery, and she did not know what secrets lurked behind his detached air. But, he did not seem a stranger to her heart. With soft, breathless excitement, Kat made up her mind. If there was any way to work her way into Jules's heart she would find it. Hannah had said she was resourceful; now she was meeting the most important challenge of her life.

Kat napped the morning away. She didn't wish to shut dear Hannah and Caroline out, but she needed this time alone, to prepare herself mentally.

After a light tea served in her chamber, Kat took a long leisurely bath in the copper hip tub, relaxing down into the bubbles as the maid washed her hair with scented soap. It was so thick it took hours to dry. Finally she remembered the trunks Dominic had brought. The maid was overwhelmed by gowns of satin, muslin, and crepe, and a new riding habit of sea green that very nearly, but not quite, matched her eyes.

Packed lovingly in one trunk was the most beautiful dress Kat had ever seen. Willy had said in her letter it had been her grandmother's presentation gown. It fit Kat to perfection. Her own mother, Bettina, had been smaller like Mariah, but Willy's letter had explained she remembered this dress from a portrait she'd seen and knew it would be perfect for Kat. And it was.

The dress was rose satin; the low, square neck and close fitting bodice were edged with fine lace. Its half sleeve was also banded in lace and finished in three tiers of ruffles. The full skirt worn over voluminous petticoats emphasized Kat's tiny waist. It was an entirely different style than Kat was used to—the straight empire lines seemed much less revealing, but if her godmother had gone to so much trouble to send it she must wear it.

Twirling around before the mirror, the petticoats brushing her legs, Kat was happy Willy had sent it. The dress made her feel like a bride. What would Jules think of it? And of her in it?

What of his brother? Dominic had seemed most forbidding. A future duke for a new brother—it was all too much to take in. But the cleric and the special license couldn't be denied. In all truth she did not wish to cry off. Tonight she would marry for love.

She had chosen for the ceremony to take place after supper, on the terrace of the château, with the beauty of the flower gardens around her. Madame Bernair had lit the garden with every available candelabrum and candlestick. It looked as if the night sky had reached down with its stars to the earth.

Jules stood in full court dress a little apart from the rest of the group. Jacko and Caroline whispered together on the stone bench. Dominic, Hannah, and the cleric were debating with the abbé which ceremony should come first—the English or the French.

Steeling her nerve she traversed the small salon and exited the château. All conversation ceased as the party saw her.

Instantly, Jules came forward, holding a velvet box. The smile that had first touched her heart softened his face. "My dear, you are even more beautiful tonight. Before we begin I would like a moment." He lifted his eyebrow, but this time it did not seem haughty or detached to her. "Kathryn, I have no betrothal ring and very little of my

105

heritage to present to you, but I hope you will wear these as a token of my regard."

He clasped a breathtaking parure of rubies around her neck. The graduated stones were linked by pounded gold and a large, pigeon egg ruby hung in the hollow between her breasts.

She was astonished at their beauty. And at the tenderness she glimpsed in his eyes.

"This belonged to my great-grandmother. My mother took it to England when we fled the terror, but never wore it for she did not care for rubies. My stepgrandmother, the Duchess of Culter, remembered and sent it for this occasion."

"It is lovely," she breathed, touching the large stone where it hung between her breasts. Already the ruby had gained warmth from her body.

Madame Bernair stepped discreetly onto the terrace and Jules asked her to have the staff, small as it was, be present to witness his marriage. In a matter of minutes the terrace was full of people.

At a nod from Dominic, Jules led her to where both the abbé and curate stood. The abbé began first, speaking so rapidly in French Kat could not make out all the words, but she followed Jules's lead; bowing her head in prayer at the appropriate moment, making her response a firm *"oui."*

Finally the abbé stepped back and the curate began the English wedding ceremony. She understood every word of this service, and when the curate reached the place in the ceremony that required them to recite their vows, Kat was afraid to raise her eyes to Jules for fear he would plainly see her feelings or that what she saw on his face would disappoint her.

At last the curate declared them man and wife and she lifted her head to meet Jules's stare.

As they had done that day in the winery, their eyes locked, and Kat was powerless to look away. That flame leapt to life in Jules's gaze and he embraced her shoulders in a powerful move, pulling her tightly to his chest. Her head fell back against his strong arms and he kissed her so deeply, so sweetly and passionately that her lips pulsed beneath his. Her arms gathered him even closer as her mouth answered his searching quest. This was what love felt like, this breathless hot excitement.

Ever so slowly he released her, stepping away, and she felt bereft. But she smiled brightly as their family rushed forward to shower them with well wishes.

Kat had just married the man she loved. His kiss had promised that all would be well between them. But she dared not reveal her heart in case she'd misread him. How uncomfortable it would be for both of them if she acknowledged her feelings and he did not share them. It would be better to live in a fantasy of her own making. Until tonight. Tonight she would discover the secret his kiss so sweetly promised.

Jules stared out the window at the full moon spreading its silvery light on his land. The château was finally quiet after the wedding party Madame Bernair had overseen. Wine from his own cellars— his father's best vintage—had flowed freely, but he had sipped very little, as had Kathryn.

Tonight he had everything he'd ever dreamed of— a beautiful woman he cared for deeply, his father's estate to leave as a heritage for the son he looked

107

forward to producing, and an estate in England, Langley Manor, not far from Culter Towers. A smaller property of the duchess's, she had deeded it as a wedding gift to him. Now he had a home in England where Kathryn might be happy.

He paced to the connecting door, nervously tugging on the tie of his robe. He knew she was there waiting for him. All day the staff had worked to get the master suite, with the sitting room and connecting bedrooms, ready for them.

If only he knew Kathryn's feelings. But how could he? He didn't even know his own. Taking a deep breath, he lifted his hand and opened the door between them.

She sat quietly before the fire, brushing her hair.

She rose, all atremble, the instant he entered. Jules had never seen anyone more beautiful. Her sun-kissed hair cascaded about her shoulders, and her heavily lashed aquamarine eyes were luminous in the soft light. He knew she could not be aware how the firelight outlined her full breasts, the curve of her waist, and the gentle slope of hip and thigh beneath the white lace negligee.

At last he had breath to speak. "Kathryn, we must talk."

He was rewarded by a small smile. "Yes. It is . . . a trifle awkward, is it not?"

Moving quickly, before he could change his mind, he joined her before the dying embers of the fire. The fragrance of her hair drew his hand to play thoughtfully amid the curls.

"Kathryn, you know I would never do anything to harm you."

"I know," she whispered.

He longed to kiss her again as he had on the terrace, but felt he didn't have the right. He had to be fair, give her time to get accustomed to their new relationship.

He studied her. Kathryn's eyes remained half-closed as if she feared to meet his gaze, and her complexion changed from milky white to a rosy glow. Then she lifted her lids and Jules was suddenly drowning in the luminous beauty of her eyes. The last vestige of doubt fled and with an enormous force of will, Jules stepped away from her.

"Do you trust me, Kathryn?"

At her eager nod he smiled. "Then sleep now, my dear," he said quietly. "It has been a long day for you. We must come to terms with our relationship. Tomorrow we will begin," he promised, his voice growing in confidence with every word.

He heard a faint little sob but dared not look back when he reached the door.

He had been wrong; there was a love match like Dominic and Juliana's for him. He was in love with Kathryn—her bravery, her spirit, her warmth. She inflamed his senses and filled his heart. Now, somehow, he must make her feel the same. Only then, in mutual love, would he make her his. But first he would return with her to London to still any trace of gossip, as Dominic had recommended. There amid her family and friends, surely she would feel more at home and be more receptive to his wooing. And wooing his beautiful wife had suddenly become the most important thing in his life.

Chapter 9

KAT STARED BLINDLY into the fireplace, tears burning her cheeks. These feelings for Jules were so fresh, so new, her world was topsy-turvy. Such a short time ago he had been a stranger, albeit a kind one, now just thinking about him made her tremble.

Rubbing her wet cheeks with her palms, Kat stood, pacing to the window. In the silvery moonlight the rolling lawns of the château melded into the vineyards and the hills beyond.

This was her wedding night.

She glanced down, carefully running her fingers over the fine lace ruffles of the negligee. Her body had burned with embarrassment when she had donned this and looked in the mirror. But the embarrassment had quickly faded to breathless anticipation.

A dry aching sob welled in her throat; she could no longer keep the truth at bay. Jules did not want her for his wife in that way. He had been forced into this marriage of convenience by her foolishness. He was so noble he was sacrificing his chance of a future love match to save her reputation.

The sweet, passionate kiss that had left her weak with new emotions and longings had meant nothing to him. It had just been a form, or perhaps a test—that she had failed.

Still a little flame of hope refused to be completely extinguished.

Kat thrust up her chin, taking a deep, ragged breath. She was not a weak-spirited young woman. She had always believed in action, and she would carry on by being an unexceptional wife to him. She now knew love found its way into one's heart quite on its own. There was no way to see it coming so there was no way to stop it. But if there was a way she could help it make its journey into Jules's heart she would discover it.

Gwynneth needed a glass of madeira, not the insipid tea Sybilla had just poured for her. But even Gwynneth didn't have the nerve to ask for such a strong drink at this early hour.

Dominic had sent word when he arrived in Northhampton that all the travelers would reach London in time for luncheon today. Mariah had insisted she be on hand for the newlyweds' arrival. She and Gwynneth had descended upon the duchess and refused to be dislodged. Mariah's eyes were dull with worry and she didn't seem quite herself today. No doubt Gwynneth looked like a hag herself. Only Sybilla appeared beautifully serene and absolutely composed.

Exasperated past bearing, Gwynneth snorted. "Really, Sybilla, how can you be so unfeeling! What if we have done the wrong thing?" Gwynneth's chest swelled in indignation.

Sybilla looked down her nose. "My dear Gwynneth, must I remind you again, that if *your* goddaughter had not been so foolish as to go to that inn unchaperoned none of this would have been necessary. My wonderful Jules is the noble victim of—"

"*Victim!*" Gwynneth roared. "He has won a priceless jewel in Kat. And, furthermore—"

"Will you two please stop bickering!" Mariah broke in, standing, her eyes flashing with anger. "The damage is done! Nothing will help now! They are married!" As if realizing she had just committed the unpardonable sin of bellowing at one of England's premier duchesses, she slowly sank back into the chair.

"You are absolutely right, of course, Mariah," Sybilla sniffed. Then lifting the dainty china tea pot, she gave Gwynneth a sweet smile, saying, "May I freshen your tea, dear Gwynneth?"

"Thank you, dear Sybilla. That would be *lovely*," Gwynneth cooed in response. They were still being disgustingly polite to each other when noises from the hallway brought them all to their feet.

Kat, dressed in one of her new frocks, a canary yellow batiste with two ruffles about the hem and a matching poke bonnet, stood for an instant in the doorway, before launching herself into Mariah's arms.

She looked the same; rich, thick, blond curls nearly tumbling from beneath the bonnet, wide Thistlewait eyes alert and twinkling, and her dimpled smile warming all, Gwynneth thought. Only when Kat turned back to the door where the rest of the party stood was she able to assess what was uppermost on her mind. Jules had eyes for no one but Kat, and when their gazes met, Gwynneth went limp with relief. It was there: that inexplicable tension, that silent connection which strong feeling gives to those so affected. It was the sign Gwynneth, secretly worried to death over the arranged marriage, had desperately hoped to see. She had been correct after all; Kat *had* fallen in love with the dashing comte.

At that moment the rest of the party surged through the door, Dominic going to Sybilla and Jacko engulfing Mariah in a huge brotherly hug. Only Hannah hung back, but curiously she was not alone. A tiny blond vision with enormous eyes surveyed the gathering with lively curiosity.

"Kathryn my dear, shouldn't you introduce your friend?" Gwynneth encouraged, pinning her goddaughter with an indulgent eye.

"Caroline, I'm sorry! In the excitement I have forgotten my manners." Kat laughed, leading the doll-like creature closer.

"Your Grace, I would like to introduce a dear friend of the family, Miss Caroline Strange of Northumberland."

Sybilla threw Gwynneth a questioning look before doing the pretty with the girl.

Friend of the family, indeed! Gwynneth, herself, had never laid eyes on the chit before. What was Kat up to now? Strange . . . from Northumberland? Tapping her finger against her lip, Gwynneth tried to recall the family.

Of course! The father was a nabob! Girl must be worth fifty thousand pounds a year if she was worth a penny. Too bad Gwynneth didn't have another godson.

"Willy and Mariah, you remember dear Caroline, do you not?" Kat asked, utterly guileless.

The child had turned into a shocking minx! But, of course, Gwynneth went right along with her, as

113

did Mariah, giving Caroline a smile and brief kiss upon her rosy cheek.

When the little vision leaned over to kiss Gwynneth's cheeks, she whispered pertly, "Thank you, Lady Tutwilliger. Kat will explain all!"

Then everyone began to speak at once, regaling the duchess with the rigors of travel, the beauty of Champagne, and how lovely the wedding by moonlight in the château garden had been.

With a sinking heart, Gwynneth noticed that Kat and Jules were oddly silent and that her goddaughter now studiously avoided looking at him. This was no shyness or the flush of new intimacy; there was something else going on here. It didn't seem to fit with the earlier look they'd shared.

This was not right, and Gwynneth would let no stone unturned until she found out what the problem was; however, right now was not the time.

Sybilla rose regally from her chair and took both Kat and Jules by their hands. The company quieted. "Jules dear, you know how meddlesome I can be, but please indulge me. I've taken the liberty of having rooms prepared for you both here. Culter House is yours for the Season. And to celebrate your marriage I am giving a ball in your honor tomorrow."

Jules quizzed his eyebrow and shrugged.

Pride swelled in Gwynneth's breast as Kat leaned over and pressed a kiss upon Sybilla's cheek before saying exactly the right thing. "We are honored, Your Grace. And I look forward to the time we shall spend together."

"And the day after tomorrow you are to have *my* box at the opera," Gwynneth piped in, not wanting to be outdone. "The sooner you two are seen to-

114

gether in public the sooner you will cease to be a nine-day wonder."

"Thank you, Lady Tutwilliger, we shall be delighted to accept your kind invitation," Jules drawled. "I relish the opportunity to further our acquaintance."

"Ho! I won't be going with you! Hate the opera! Thought I'd send Jacko," Gwynneth finished, delighted to see the look of horror descend upon her godson's stunning countenance. Really, the boy deserved it after what he'd put them through. If he hadn't decided to hare off to the Continent, none of this would have happened!

Jacko opened his mouth in protest, but stopped seeing Caroline's enraptured face.

"Oh, how wonderful! The opera . . ." she breathed, periwinkle blue eyes glowing with excitement.

"Like the opera, do you, Miss Strange?" Jacko asked, an odd little smile curving his mouth.

"Oh, yes, it is quite my favorite thing. But I have not had the opportunity to attend here in London," she answered wistfully.

"Well, you shall attend tomorrow . . . with me!" he declared proudly, much to Gwynneth's utter and complete shock.

Oh, stuff and nonsense! Her well-organized plans were collapsing around her! Gwynneth had everything set in her mind: Kat and Jules, Mariah and Christian, Jacko and Helen. Now, however, she could plainly see she must find someone else for Miss Helen Vanderworth!

Jules stared at the dark oak door connecting his rooms to Kathryn's. It had remained firmly closed last night. Today had been completely taken up with his solicitor concerning Château Saville and Langley Manor, plus certain inquiries into the whereabouts of Sir Edmund Trigge. If the bounder was in London he would soon know Jules was looking for him. A few words in the right place and Sir Edmund would no longer be welcomed by anyone that mattered. He knew Kathryn had been busy all day getting Caroline settled at Lady Tutwilliger's. By his design they had not met.

He dressed for the ball in his usual severe black-and-white garb, but, for tonight, did add a diamond stickpin, a gift from the duke, to his cravat. He stepped out into the hall just in time to see the duchess begin to descend the stairs.

"*Grandmère*, may I escort you," he called, hurrying to tuck her hand into the curve of his arm. "I tried to see you earlier but your maid said you were napping."

"My dear boy, you look positively dashing tonight." She smiled, winking at him. "Between you and Dominic, you do me proud."

"I'm sorry Dominic couldn't be here tonight, but I understand his eagerness to return to Juliana."

The duchess shot him a shrewd look and no wonder, he had even been able to hear the wistful tone in his voice.

"I have done the right thing for you, haven't I, my boy?"

Reaching the foyer where they would greet their guests, Jules lifted her fragile fingers to his lips. "Your kindness to me has always known no bounds. But to gift me with Langley Manor is beyond words. I told Dominic I could not accept it, but he would have no part of that."

"As well he shouldn't! Austin would be here himself to reassure you if he had not remained with Juliana. It was always our plan to give it to you. There is more than enough property for all our family."

Kissing her cheek, Jules smiled. "It means I shall always have a home near those I love."

As if satisfied with his words, she nodded. "It is what Austin, Dominic, and I wished. For you to have the happiness that will, at last, put all the dark memories to rest. Can Kathryn give you that peace, my dear?"

Jules did not answer for a slight rustle at the top of the stairs caused them both to turn and look up. Then words were not necessary.

Kathryn paused on the top step. She wore a deep rose crepe gown cut low across her breasts, exposing more of that creamy flesh than Jules had ever seen, except on their wedding night when he had forced himself to leave her quickly while he had still been able to do so.

Slowly, she descended the stairs. Jules went to take her hand to lead her forward. Only then did he see that she wore the Devereaux rubies.

Seeing his pleasure, she touched the rich, red stones. "They are perfect with this gown, and I enjoy wearing them, for you." Her eyes begged for reassurance.

That timidity was not Kat's usual style. What could she be worried about, looking so delectable? It must be concern for their first appearance in public since the wedding. He wished to banish all uncertainty from her beautiful eyes and replace it with something else indeed. Lifting both her hands, he turned them up and pressed a kiss into each

117

palm. Slowly, carefully, he fully intended to seduce his beautiful wife.

Tonight was the beginning.

Peering up into her suddenly flushed face, he smiled. "The jewels only enhance your perfection, Kathryn," he murmured, but was struck speechless by his own internal response to the widening of her aquamarine eyes and the gasp that escaped from her soft lips.

"Now, children, stop flirting, our guests are arriving," the duchess teased, warning them just a moment before the butler opened the door.

Hours later, the last guest finally greeted, Jules led the duchess and Kathryn into the crowded ballroom. The ton was sipping champagne as they wandered through the upstairs and out onto the terrace. Steps led back down into the gardens, which due to the duchess's passion for horticulture, rivaled those at Culter Towers. Tonight, lanterns were strung through the garden, and there was no doubt in Jules's mind that anyone intent on dalliance would make his way out there.

A sudden thought made him glance down at Kathryn. She was smiling up at him, the dimples deep in her soft cheeks.

"It is lovely, isn't it? You may not have noticed but the duchess wishes us to begin the dance."

It was the first time he had held Kathryn in his arms like this and he found it utterly delightful; they fit together perfectly, their steps matching as they glided to the strains of the waltz. He had the most absurd desire to tug lose the wreath of flowers that held her curls up and let her hair tumble about her shoulders as it had on their wedding night.

Not even newlyweds could be excused such behavior; he resisted the impulse to bury his fingers in her rich curls and tip back her head so he could press kisses down her smooth, white throat.

Other couples joined them on the floor, and Jules was glad for the diversion. His body was betraying his thoughts, and he must in no way frighten his young wife. Early on he had recognized her daring spirit and her sense of adventure, but these waters, he instinctively knew, were new to her.

Having lost Kathryn to several smitten young noblemen who filled her dance card, he leaned against the wall, content to watch her cut a graceful figure in the dance. He surveyed the party. As usual, the duchess had drawn all the best of Society and was entertaining them handsomely. She and a turbaned Lady Tutwilliger held court with the dowagers at the far end of the ballroom. Mariah, breathtakingly lovely in a silk gown of deepest blue, glided by in the arms of a tall, distinguished man Jules did not recognize. He did, however, know the couple arguing, not too quietly, near a potted plant off to his left.

"Oh, I don't believe you! You just don't wish to waltz!" Very nearly, Caroline stamped her slipper clad foot, but instead marched up to Jules.

He bowed. "Good evening, Miss Strange."

"Oh, Count, is it true Lord Thistlewait cannot waltz with me because we have not been formally introduced?" She fumed. "That is perfectly absurd because we have been traveling together for weeks."

Jules shot Jacko an apologetic look. "I believe that only applies to Almack's," he drawled.

"Oh, I knew it!" she gushed triumphantly.

"Dash it, I'm no good at this." Jacko pouted, but

nonetheless led the determined Miss Strange onto the dance floor. Jules noticed that within a very few minutes she had him at ease and when next they glided by, Jacko was doing a tolerable job and was even laughing at something Caroline was saying.

To Jules's delight when the waltz ended Kathryn appeared to search the crowd for him. She hurried to his side.

"Can it be that this is finally my dance, Madame Countess?" he asked, placing her hand on his arm.

Sighing, she turned him toward the terrace. "The countess needs some fresh air. Would you mind forgoing our country dance?"

Chuckling, he shook his head, effortlessly guiding her through the throng to the dimly lit terrace. He couldn't quite believe his luck; all evening he had been plotting how to get his young wife out into the moonlight, and now she had suggested it herself.

"I believe there is a gazebo down the path to our right. Would you care to see it?" he felt as nervous as a schoolboy.

"That would be lovely," she sighed again. "Perhaps we could sit there for a few moments and enjoy the night."

The bench in the gazebo was barely large enough for two, especially when Kathryn turned sideways and tilted her face upward.

"Jules, would you mind very much, but I think something flew into my eye." Blinking her long lashes, she gazed up at him.

Cradling her face in his hands, he studiously examined each beautiful eye; they were wide, clear, and deep enough to drown in.

"I don't see anything, Kathryn," he said slowly.

She fluttered her lashes a few times. "There, I think it is better."

Jules couldn't help himself. He kissed her eyelids, her long lashes feathering his lips. Then he brushed her high cheekbone with his searching mouth, and when she gave a breathless sigh he caught it with his lips in a long caressing kiss. He felt her body yield its softness to his, and his mouth moved hungrily to the curve of her throat. Carefully, he repressed his body's desires; with Kathryn he must go slow.

A woman's laughter broke them apart; a couple was coming down the path toward them. Kathryn stared at him, her eyes sparkling like jewels in the moonlight. He pressed a brief kiss on her sweet lips one last time. "I believe it is about to become crowded in here. Shall we go in?"

She was uncharacteristically quiet on the way back into the house, but really there was no need for words. Jules was more determined than ever that very soon the connecting door between their rooms would be permanently open.

Kathryn stared at herself in the mirror. Did she look all right? She was wearing another low-cut gown; this one in her favorite color of sea-foam green. And tonight for the opera she had allowed one fat curl to fall over her shoulder and onto the curve of her breast. Was she being too obvious? Had last night's ploy of wishing for some fresh air been too blatant? Perhaps pretending something had gotten into her eye had been a bit much. But these were new waters for Kat; she didn't know how to go about seducing someone, let alone her husband. She was simply acting by instinct. She twirled, checking every detail of her costume in the mirror and smiled secretly to herself. Her actions had had the desired effect. Jules was not totally immune to her charms. When he had held her and kissed her in the gazebo she had experienced the most remarkable sensations. Warmth had flooded through her; she'd felt like she was floating in a sea of new, wonderful emotions. If she had anything to say about it, she determined to her reflection, tonight would hold even more such delights!

Jules waited for her in the foyer, his black evening cape swirling around him as he turned to her. She experienced that breathless anticipation again when he gazed up at her and smiled.

"You look lovely tonight, Kathryn, as always. That color very nearly matches your eyes," he complimented.

Kat shivered as his fingers brushed her bare shoulders when he placed her dark velvet cape lined in the same sea-foam green satin about her.

She moved quickly away so he wouldn't notice, still unsure of her tactics around him. "Have Jacko and Caroline not arrived yet?"

"They have gone ahead in the first carriage. Come, we shall miss the curtain."

He handed her up into a large, crested town carriage and climbed in beside her, sliding his arm along the seat back. His fingers began to absently stroke the curl falling down her throat.

"I like your hair like this, Kathryn," he drawled, seemingly intent on the movement of his hand.

Kat was feeling decidedly warm. If only he would look at her, perhaps then he might kiss her again. Shocked at her thoughts at such an inappropriate moment, right here in the street, a hot flush crept up her neck and face.

It was a relief when the carriage stopped, for Kat was having difficulty breathing with Jules so near.

With him as guide they made their way smoothly to Lady Tutwilliger's box. Caroline was already seated at the front with Jacko behind her. To Kat's surprise, Jacko did not appear peevish as he usually did when called upon to do something he disliked. Instead, he was eagerly leaning forward, listening to Caroline's chatter.

"Oh, look, there are the Duke and Duchess of York. And there is Lady Sefton. Oh, Kathryn, come sit down! Everyone has been looking up at our box."

"Then let us give them something beautiful to look at," Jules drawled, drawing her forward. "Smile, my dear, remember what your godmother told us. The sooner the ton gets their fill of us, the sooner we shall cease being a novelty." With that, he lifted her fingers to his lips for all the world to see.

She did not have to pretend to be a loving wife in return. If only he wasn't pretending, she speculated as he seated her and pulled his chair close enough that his arm rested near her.

She could hardly keep her mind on the music because of his nearness. Drifting between the love story being enacted on the stage and thoughts of her own romantic predicament, she was startled when the house lights went up at the end of the first act. She blinked in confusion. There was a great hubbub as the patrons filed out to the foyer. But, Kat suddenly noticed that one woman in the box directly across the theater was staring at her quite intensely. Kat didn't recognize her. She was lushly beautiful, with blond hair falling daringly about her bare shoulders. The woman tilted her head to speak to someone behind her and when the man leaned forward Kat gasped. Sir Edmund Trigge!

"What is it, Kathryn?" Jules inquired, then followed her stunned gaze. She felt him go rigid beside her.

She turned to him with wide eyes. "Did you see him, Jules? Sir Edmund."

"Where?" he bit out.

"In the box across from us." Frowning, she shook her head. "I thought you saw him, too."

He stood purposefully. "Don't be concerned, Kathryn. I will handle this."

She rose to stop him but he was already out of their box and lost in the throng promenading in the hallway.

"Is something wrong, Kat?" her twin, engrossed in conversation with Caroline, finally took notice of her.

"Of course not," she laughed. "Why don't you take Caroline for an orangeade? You might bring me back a glass."

"Are you sure you'll be all right here alone?"

"Go, silly!" she insisted. "Jules will be returning any moment."

But he didn't come back. The moments lengthened into minutes. Kat stared intently at the box across the theater. The woman had gone and there was no sign of Sir Edmund. Had she imagined it was him? Truth to tell, the lighting had been dim. Maybe she had conjured him out of shadows.

The door opened, and she twirled in relief. Slowly she rose to her feet in surprise. The lovely blond woman, who at closer range seemed much older and more sophisticated, stood in the doorway. She smiled, her gaze searching the box.

"I am so sorry, but I just had to see my dear friend, Jules. But it appears I have missed him."

"May I help you? I am the Countess Saville." It was the first time Kat had used the title, and it sounded strange to her.

Obviously it sounded strange to the woman also, because a rather hard look came over her soft mouth. "Yes, so I have been informed. When last I saw Jules he did not mention you," she stated baldly.

Kat was shocked. She wasn't so green that she couldn't guess what kind of friendship Jules had with this woman. That she should confront Jules's wife and in so obvious a way was unheard of. Kat had been raised to deal with every social situation; confronting a mistress could be no different, say, than dealing with a pushy tradesman.

She thrust up her chin. "Although our acquaintance was long-standing Jules had patience only for a brief engagement before our marriage. You are with Sir Edmund Trigge I see," Kat stated boldly and was rewarded with a cool smile.

"Yes, the three of us, Jules, Sir Edmund, and I spent much time together in Rome last year. . . ."

Having confirmed that it was indeed Sir Edmund, Kat could not bear to speak to this creature another moment. "I shall tell my husband you stopped by. I am sorry, but I didn't get your name?"

Tossing back her head, the creature smiled in such a way that Kat wanted to scratch her eyes out.

"Tell him Contessa Marietta Louisa Primavetta is most eager to renew his . . . acquaintance."

"Good evening." Kat dismissed the other woman. Trembling, she sank slowly into her chair. How sure the contessa must be of Jules to so blatantly make an appearance. Kat knew that wives did not give their husbands messages from their mistresses. This would be another secret she would keep to herself, just as she was keeping silent about Sir Edmund's threats.

There was no doubt in her mind he had been behind the contessa's little visit. As much as she hated to admit it, Sir Edmund had accomplished his task; Kat was frightened. He seemed to know where she was vulnerable. First, Jacko; now, Jules.

Suddenly, Kat's plan to somehow seduce her husband into loving her seemed very young and foolish. How could she compete for a heart? Kat wiped away a tear with her lace handkerchief. She must be composed before Jules returned. Not by a flicker of her eyelashes would she let it be known that her heart now possessed a small crack.

Chapter 10

KAT HAD SPENT another sleepless night, alone in her room at Culter House. It was now patently obvious that Jules could have little or no regard for her. Why that should pain her so was a well-guarded secret that she would forever keep hidden in a tiny corner of her heart. Pride demanded that she not push herself upon him any more than she had already.

As much as she longed to lie in bed, pulling not only the lavender-scented sheets but also the heavy silk bedcover over her head, there was work to be done. The duchess was a darling, once you got used to her strident tongue, and Kat felt obligated not to be a burden on her household.

She wished Jules would move them out of London as fast as possible! Then perhaps no one need ever see her private heartbreak.

The manor house the duke and duchess had so generously deeded to them sounded a perfect retreat. There at least she could keep occupied with running the staff and managing the household. Even the little taste she'd had at the château had whetted her appetite for more.

Her house would be as efficiently run as this one, she decided, running lightly down the steps. As forthright as the duchess was, no one had ever heard her berate a servant. And the staff adored her.

The under-house parlor maid had already trimmed the lamps and candles and straightened the formal salon. Kat wandered back toward the kitchens. It was too early for breakfast, and she was restless. The chef, preparing cutlets for Jules's delight, was scandalized when Kat entered his domain.

"I wish only to see how your kitchen functions," Kat apologized, then added ingenuously, "Someday I will have to know all these things myself."

She must have spoken the magic words for Gaston immediately unbent and Kat spent a delightful hour perched on a wooden chair, hastily brought from the servant's dining hall, observing and commenting on her surroundings. When she could delay there no longer she went to the morning room where she planned to write a long introductory letter to her new sister-in-law.

Fate, which seemed to be popping up with alarming regularity in her life, intervened. Jules, looking as if he hadn't yet been to bed since they returned from the opera last night, was rummaging through a drawer. His cravat had been loosened, and his clothes were rumpled. He stopped short when Kat entered.

"Kathryn . . ." he took a step toward her. "What do you here so early?"

"I'm sorry to disturb you, my lord," she returned most correctly. "I thought perhaps I could take care of some correspondence. However, I do not wish to bother you. . . ."

They had dealt together much better than this in

128

France before they were married. As they had dealt well here until last night. Kat felt the veriest green schoolgirl! She had honestly believed she could capture this dashing man's heart and make him wish for no one else, just as her parents had loved.

He stiffened, just as he had done upon returning to the box to find Kat had withdrawn to treat him like a distant stranger. Really! she thought. It was nigh impossible to deal with men and their peccadilloes, but it was the outside of enough when they made a woman feel it was her fault!

Where was the kind friend of the boat? The entertaining companion at the château? The vulnerable brave man who needed her when they had been attacked? The gentle man who had stood before her, making her wedding fears disappear? That was the Jules she had fallen in love with; still loved, even though he might not be faithful to their wedding vows. That thought was so painful she blinked rapidly, stepping away from him. If he wished to have a marriage with her in name only, well, two could play at that game.

"I must be off, then." She waved one hand languidly. "I believe I'll spend the day with my sister and godmother. There's no need to disturb yourself."

She flew up the stairs before Jules could have a chance to reply, or to see the tears threatening in her burning eyes.

"Damnation!" Jules said it aloud. Since last night she had become another person, brittle and distant. What had he done? He had racked his brain all night and still come up empty. This was not his Kat, full of warmth and fire. What could have changed her in those few minutes? He knew he shouldn't have left her at all, but the shock of seeing Marietta was so great he had to make inquiries. Even though their liaison had ended amicably when he came home to England over a year ago, he wasn't pleased she had turned up just now. And with Edmund Trigge. That made her appearance in London, which she heartily detested because of the dampness, particularly worrisome. What new mischief might Trigge plot? Jules couldn't be certain how Kat might react now that she was behaving so peculiarly.

Had he been too forward, kissing her in the gazebo? In all honesty he couldn't help himself that she had been so appealing. Had he frightened her with his advances? On their wedding night he'd thought he was doing the right thing, being understanding, giving her time to know him. Nothing was working out the way he'd planned.

He'd never have what Dominic had with his Juliana because Kat did not love him. He'd been a fool to believe they were growing closer and that in time she'd come to care for him. Care for him! Damnation, that wasn't what he yearned for! He wished for her to feel the burning ache that tortured him whenever he was near her. He would not rest until he won her heart. This was simply a momentary setback he determined grimly.

Perhaps if he could take her to the manor house. They'd be in the country; they could recapture the feelings he knew had begun in France. Then, too, they would be closer to Dominic and Juliana. Maybe if Kat could experience their relationship . . . she would want it for herself. But, he could never take her from the gaiety of London at the height of the

Season. She reveled in this—it was her world. How could he, practically a stranger, take her away from her only family and friends?

He raked long, frustrated fingers through his hair. It was nearly impossible for him to live here much longer. His grandmother, he never thought of her any other way even though they truly were not related, had given Kathryn and him a lovely suite. Unfortunately it wasn't big enough, the house wasn't big enough, he was beginning to think the city wasn't big enough . . . he couldn't be this close to Kathryn and not desire her. That was why he had gone to White's all night, not playing, hardly listening to all that went on around him, just trying with all his willpower to stay away from her.

There was only one thing for it—he had to keep himself so occupied he would have no time to think of her. He sat at the writing desk, quickly penned two notes and summoned a footman to deliver them.

An hour later found him working up a sweat at the establishment named for Gentleman Jackson. Jacko and a group of his friends watched open-mouthed as Jules went three rounds with the esteemed proprietor.

"My brother-in-law, the Comte de Saville," Jacko proudly introduced him later. "Didn't know you went in for this sort of thing."

Jules gave him an enigmatic smile. "Just brushing up my technique a bit. It never hurts to keep on top of things."

Jacko asked him to join his friends for a ride in the park, but Jules murmured something about a business appointment, so Jacko went merrily off. It was just as well, Jules wasn't fit company for any-one. Not even himself.

It was worse luck to run into Marietta on Bond Street. After all the years they had known each other, he could not cut her. As it was, she came up right beside him.

"I received your note about Sir Edmund. Thank you for warning me, *caro*." She shrugged, batting her darkened eyelashes. "He was always only barely acceptable at best."

"Then why were you at the opera with him last night?" Jules asked coolly.

"*Caro*, you know I have few acquaintances in London," she pouted. "And now that you are mar-ried, I suppose we—"

"You are correct, Marietta," he lifted his eye-brow. "We ended as friends, I would like to keep that memory."

"You know I wish that, too." Suddenly she lifted a hand to her eyes. "This terrible English damp. I have the most shocking headache. Would you help me to my carriage? It is just down the street."

Jules could not be so ungallant as to leave Mar-ietta ill in the middle of the street so he allowed her to tuck her hand into his arm as they made their way to her carriage.

She brightened slightly as he helped her in. "*Caro*, I will try to stay out of your way, and your wife's, too. She is a spirited young woman, is she not?"

"How would you know that, Marietta?" he ques-tioned, rejecting the idea that somehow, some-where, they might have met.

"One knows these things," she returned with a wave of her hand. "*Ciao, caro.*"

With a slight feeling of relief Jules watched her carriage disappear into the traffic. Glancing around, he was pleased to see no one he knew. With everything else that was going wrong, all he needed was some rattle carrying this tale to his beautiful, exasperating wife.

Kathryn had wasted hours on her toilette. She'd heard Jules come and go from their suite without making the least push to see her. Then she'd spent far too long deciding over unimportant purchases at the Pantheon Bazaar. Finally it was eleven o'clock, and, she felt reasonably sure, a civilized hour for a newly married lady to pay a call on her very own sister without raising too much speculation on the subject of her marriage.

Unfortunately, she turned into Bond Street just in time to see the contessa strolling arm in arm, and looking very cozy, with Jules. For once, she so far forgot herself as to urge her horse forward into traffic, uncaring of the other drivers around her.

She had worked herself into a fine snit by the time she arrived at Lady Tutwilliger's town house. Insisting that her maid hold the reins while she informed Westley to have a footman take her carriage round to the mews was entirely uncharacteristic behavior. The scandalized maid was only too happy to escape to the kitchen.

Willy was holding court in the dining room with a listless Mariah and a resigned, albeit attentive, Hannah Hamilton.

"Where is Caroline?" Kat asked, stripping off her gloves and settling into the chair Westley pulled out for her.

"Jacko came by with two of his cohorts and took

her for a ride in the park. I sent along a maid, of course," Lady Tutwilliger sniffed, favoring Kat with a piercing look. "When are we going to have that little chat you promised me?"

Kat should have known Willy could not be fobbed off when she wanted to know something. Since the day they arrived back in London, Willy had wanted to know about Kat's marriage. Yesterday Kat could honestly have told her godmother that she was happy, but not today, so she changed the subject.

"Mariah dear, you look pale," Kat said, noticing that in all truth her beautiful sister did look decidedly ill.

"It is my tooth. It is killing me," she murmured, cupping the offending jaw with her fingers.

"You need a dose of laudanum," Hannah stated matter-of-factly. "I often use it for the same problem. It will do the trick, I promise you."

"Then let us get some now," Mariah cried, rising to her feet. "I cannot take more of this pain."

Making soothing noises Hannah shepherded a slumped-shouldered Mariah from the room.

Flicking her godmother an apologetic smile, Kat followed them. "I'll be back as soon as she is settled."

An hour later, Mariah was tucked cozily under the covers, peacefully asleep with the help of the laudanum. As promised Kat rejoined her godmother who had moved to the salon to receive visitors.

"Mariah is sleeping now," Kat informed her godmother before she began to roam restlessly about the room.

"Do sit down! I promise not to quiz you. It is obvious to even the meanest intellect that you do not wish to talk. Besides, we have a more immediate problem!" Willy declared with a look of doom.

"What is it?" Kat asked, happy to be able to deal with anyone else's problems. She slipped down beside Willy on the couch.

"It is your sister and Mr. Vanderworth. The wretched man is no closer to declaring himself than ever. They were to ride together today, now what do I tell him?"

"The truth. Mariah has the toothache." Kat shrugged, not really seeing the problem.

"Don't be a peagoose! A toothache indeed! The truth is totally unacceptable." Willy's foot tapped in rhythm with her finger upon her pursed lips. There was a decided gleam in her eyes that Kat found alarming. She had seen it before and bedlam usually followed.

Promptly fifteen minutes later, Mr. Vanderworth presented himself for his ride with Mariah. He was as correct as ever, black Hessians gleaming and his cravat tied to perfection. How could Mariah be drawn to this stony-faced man whom Kat had never seen express any emotion besides the barest smile?

"Mr. Vanderworth, it is *delightful* to see you, but I'm afraid Mariah is unable to ride with you today," Willy sighed mournfully.

Was there a spark of emotion in those eyes? And, yes, Kat did see a faint flush on his chiseled cheeks!

"I hope nothing is amiss?" he inquired politely.

Willy lifted a handkerchief to her eyes, but not before she had flashed Kat a quelling look.

"We don't know . . . yet. The physician is on his way."

"The physician! Is it that serious?"

Kat nearly jumped at the force of his voice and

watched in fascination as Mr. Vanderworth's cool facade melted before her eyes.

"There is no way . . ." Willy tried to continue.

"The king's physician must be called in!" He jumped to his feet and paced the salon. "He is the best in the land. Mariah must have the best care possible!"

"I really don't think the king's physician is necessary," Willy offered timidly.

"Not necessary! Of course it is! I insist upon it!" He nearly shouted, his eyes wild with concern.

"You insist, Mr. Vanderworth?" Willy asked softly with a self-satisfied smile upon her face.

"Lady Tutwilliger, surely you have not failed to notice my regard for Lady Mariah. This is possibly not the time, but . . ."

Willy stopped his eager attempts with the lift of her hand. "Tomorrow you might speak to Lord Thistlewait. Nine o'clock sharp."

"Yes, yes, of course," he nodded backing from the room. "Please send me a note after the doctor calls. I shall be waiting."

"Of course, dear boy. The instant we know!" Willy promised, gently smiling as a shaken Mr. Vanderworth took his leave.

"Willy, you are shameless," Kat scolded, unable to keep herself from chuckling.

"I know. Isn't it wonderful!" Willy beamed and was still very pleased with herself when Jacko and Caroline entered the room a few minutes later.

"Saw Vanderworth on the front steps. Why is he calling on me tomorrow?" Jacko laughed with a knowing smile.

"To ask for your sister's hand, of course! Is it not exactly what dear Mariah wished for!"

136

"Oh, how wonderful for her," Caroline sighed, before giving Kat's cheek a warm kiss. "She confided to me that she had a particular fondness for Mr. Vanderworth."

"Particular fondness! Sounds like something Mariah would say!" Jacko scoffed in true brotherly fashion. "Saw Saville at Gentleman Jackson's, Kat. Asked him to ride in park, but he said he had business."

For a few minutes all Kat's problems had disappeared, but with Jacko's words they all came rushing back. Business indeed!

Chapter 11

JULES HAD SUFFERED through two musicales, one ball, and three dinner parties in the last week, and the strain was beginning to show. After ruining his third neckcloth, he threw it to the floor in disgust. He could not bear another evening of Kathryn's cool, civilized behavior; she was at all times absolutely correct and at social events she played the part of the new bride to perfection. Even when they danced she managed to gaze up at him with a certain amount of adoration. If he didn't know better, he would have been fooled, as the ton was, declaring them a perfect match.

His grandmother appeared pleased with the outcome of her stratagem. Lady Tutwilliger, flown with success, would further her coup by announcing Mariah's engagement to Mr. Vanderworth at a ball on the morrow.

But tonight would be more of the same pretence he'd been forced to endure all week. Another sad crush at Lady Sefton's. Hardly the place to try to talk to Kathryn and unravel the mystery of her sudden change of heart. But evenings were the only times he saw her, and she made certain they were always surrounded by company. All his other attempts: at breakfast, lunch, even tea had fallen lamentably flat. She was never about. Where was she spending her time?

That thought consumed his every waking moment. The door between their rooms remained locked. In desperation, hearing noises in her room one afternoon, he'd knocked. But it was only the maid tidying her chamber. She informed him, quite cheerily, that Madame had gone to see the Elgin marbles with her brother and his friends. Jules had been unable to resist driving by the museum at a time they might be exiting. All to no avail—he missed them entirely, then spent the remainder of the day berating himself for acting the schoolboy.

He had stopped his search for Trigge who appeared, like the lowlife he was, to have gone to ground.

Looking in the mirror, Jules sighed, picked up another pristine neckcloth and proceeded to do a credible job with the Waterfall; for luck he even tucked the diamond stickpin from his grandfather in its folds. He remembered he had been wearing it that evening in the gazebo with Kathryn. Jules was not usually prone to such flights of fancy, but with his wayward bride he was finding all the old rules had flown out the window.

Lifting his brow, he gave his reflection a rueful smile. There was one thing that had not changed: his determination. It might take time—God knew how much longer he could stay away from her!— but Kathryn would once again melt in his arms as she had that night he lured her to the gazebo.

"And that I promise!" he declared fiercely, startling his valet so much, that good man left a fingerprint on the left boot he'd been buffing to perfection.

Kathryn stared at her reflection in the full-length glass that stood in the corner of her room. This dress of white crepe with a crimson overskirt demanded the rubies. She lifted the necklace and held it in her fingers. Dare she wear it? The last time had been the duchess's ball when she had shamelessly lured Jules out into the gazebo, but so much had changed since then. A fresh wave of pained betrayal dimmed her eyes, but blinking rapidly, she kept the tears at bay. Kat wasn't sure how much more of this she could endure. She'd kept herself ridiculously busy the last week. Day after day, shopping with Caroline and Mariah, indulging Jacko's mad expeditions to anywhere—as long as they kept her away from Culter House. No doubt Willy thought she had run mad, always popping in over there, demanding they be off again. The evenings she could not avoid Jules. His presence made her pulse beat more rapidly and filled her with such conflicting emotions she didn't know whether she was coming or going. It wasn't fair that he should affect her so, when she knew he did not care for her.

She sighed and clasped the necklace about her throat. Tonight she had the jitters, an odd feeling in her stomach. She'd been at Lady Sefton's the night she'd gotten Jacko's note . . . which had set her life on this course. But no doubt tonight would be totally uneventful, only another sad crush.

If Lady Sefton's musicale had been a success, this ball was doubly so. Kat had lost sight of Jules and the duchess immediately after they entered the ballroom. Although Jules was making a push to keep her by his side, demanding her dance card and promptly claiming all the waltzes, she had been pulled off by Caroline, who required her instant attention, then promptly deserted her when Jacko appeared.

Jacko dancing! And seeming to enjoy it. Caroline was turning him up sweet. She noticed Mariah with Christian Vanderworth, looking positively radiant. They appeared every inch the devoted couple. But appearances could be deceiving, Kat knew, for she often caught Jules gazing at her with a certain expression on his face that made her heart skip a beat. He was pretending for the ton, because if he truly cared for her he would not have taken up with his former mistress.

Disturbed by the feelings her thoughts evoked, Kat absently took a glass of champagne from a waiter and wandered away from the ballroom. The foyer was crammed with guests. Kat was stopped again and again by acquaintances, so it was quite some time before she made her way to the antechamber door. She knew this room was sometimes used for a rendezvous so she opened the door with some trepidation and breathed a sigh of relief on finding it empty. The quiet beckoned to her; for just a moment she would indulge herself. She sat down on the couch. As always, when Jules was nearby, her thoughts were chaotic. She'd been avoiding the problem—she needed time to think, to plan.

The tiny room was furnished with nothing but the red velvet couch. Hardly a romantic setting. Could the memory of that night, which now seemed so long ago, have drawn her here? What if she hadn't stumbled upon Sir Edmund and Caroline in this very room; probably she would not have gotten involved on the packet boat. Thus Sir Edmund would not have threatened them all, and Kat would not have lingered at Jules's château. If she had not stayed, would she have fallen in love with Jules? One thought suddenly crystalized: she had always been meant to fall in love with Jules. From that first moment on the bed at the Blue Boar Inn it was fated. Now what was she to do?

Her mind was so filled with Jules that when the antechamber door slowly opened her heart beat quickened, sure that her thoughts had called him to her. Then her heart stopped for a breathless moment. When it began to beat its fast pace had an entirely different cause.

Sir Edmund Trigge, his mouth twisted in a smug smile, clicked the door shut behind him.

Quickly, Kat rose to her feet. "What do you want?" she demanded, thrusting up her chin.

"Why, to have another of our delightful conversations," he drawled in that hated oily voice.

"I assure you that is not my wish," Kat declared, moving toward the door.

He refused to step aside to allow her to pass so Kat was forced to retreat. He followed her, that terrible smile growing more threatening.

"I've been watching you, you know, Countess."

"Oh, really? How surprising. I thought you *de trop* at most ton gatherings, Sir Edmund," she retorted with more bravado than she truly felt.

Scarlet stained his cheeks and the smile turned into a sneer. "You and Saville think you've been so damn clever, don't you! Well, I'm here to tell you I'm not finished with you yet! You might have vanquished Marietta, but not *me*, my pet." He chuckled, flicking her cheek with his finger.

His touch repulsed her, but his words brought her up short. Marietta vanquished? How? When?

Throwing back her head, she met his glare bravely. "Really, Sir Edmund, such an ineffectual ploy to throw the contessa at Jules's head." Kat shrugged dismissingly. "She and Jules were a thing of the past, long before we met."

"So it appears, but it was worth a try." He laughed harshly. "Jules thinks he can ruin me over your so-unfortunate encounter with footpads in Champagne. But I can hurt him even more. See how easily I got to you, Countess," he boasted with quivering excitement, moving so close she caught the scent of sour wine on his breath.

Sick to her stomach, Kat covered her mouth with her hand, moving back, no longer able to maintain her bravado.

"Yes, Kat, be frightened. I owe both you and Jules. And I'm a man who always gets even." He reached out to touch her again just as Kat opened her mouth to scream.

"*Don't touch her!* This is between you and me! Let us settle the score here and now, Trigge!" Jules stood in the doorway looking for all the world like an avenging dark angel.

Sir Edmund whirled in surprise to confront him. In that instant Kat sank slowly onto the bench. She wasn't so much weak with relief that Jules had come to her rescue, but prostrate with the realization that she had just spent the most miserable week of her life for nothing. Nothing! Jules had not renewed his association with the contessa. Whatever she had seen, she had misunderstood. How could she regain the comfortable relationship they had just begun to enjoy?

Edmund's drawl broke into her thoughts. "What do you propose we do, Saville? Duel here and now at Lady Sefton's? A first, no doubt," Sir Edmund preened in satisfaction. "Not sure even your vaunted relatives could cover up such a scandal. Particularly when your wife and I have been in this room alone for quite some time."

"Not a duel," Jules drawled, striding forward. "This!" he bit out, landing a punch on Sir Edmund's slack jaw. Trigge crumpled to the floor at Kat's feet, and she hastily removed her skirt from his vicinity.

With a grunt, Edmund struggled to one knee before launching himself at Jules. Both men fell to the floor, rolling over and over, fists flailing, until they came to a halt against the curtained wall. Kat looked around for some weapon, anything to help, but could find nothing, and was reduced to hated helplessness.

Finally Jules rose, lifted his opponent by his shirt front and landed one more jaw-cracking blow before letting him fall limply to the floor.

Breathing deeply, Jules turned to her, the diamond still winking in the center of his cravat. His lean face was flushed from exertion, but as yet no bruise marred his skin. With long fingers he brushed back his mussed hair and flicked his slightly askew coat into place. "I believe, Kathryn, it might be wise if we took our leave. Come," he demanded, extending his arm. "We must find the duchess before she misses us and sends up an alarm."

Wordlessly, Kat tucked her trembling fingers into the curve of his arm, threw one last look at Sir Edmund moaning on the floor, and allowed her husband to escort her from the room.

Somehow, Jules guided her through the crush, found the duchess holding court in the midst of the dowagers, soothed Lady Tutwilliger's alarm at their early retirement, and got them all into the coach before Kat could think of a word to say. It wasn't shock at what she had just witnessed so much as a total inability to make conversation with Jules's stony facade. Even his grandmother was forced into an inhabitual quietness by his stern refusal to discuss their abrupt departure.

The moment they arrived at Culter House Jules stalked into the library, closing the door firmly behind him.

The duchess faced Kat squarely. "I believe this is something to be settled between the two of you. But I will not allow you to hurt my grandson any further. If that is your intent I shall march into that room with you," she declared with brutal frankness. "It has not escaped my notice that there has been a strain between you two this past week. Whatever it is, Jules is worth fighting to keep, Kathryn."

Even though the duchess was glaring at her with her most haughty visage, Kat wasn't in the slightest undone. They *had* been at odds all week and apparently for nothing but her own foolishness. It was up to her to rectify the situation.

"I assure you, Your Grace, that I shall do everything in my power to make Jules happy," Kat said with such feeling her voice caught.

She was rewarded by an embrace; her first. "My dear girl, you have no idea what this means to me!" Stepping back, Jules's grandmother gave her an-

145

other commanding look. "Well, go on. He's been pouting in there long enough!"

Jules wasn't exactly pouting, Kat found when she stepped noiselessly into the library. He was sprawled in the wing chair with a decanter of brandy in one hand and a half-empty glass in the other. She was nearly to him before he glanced up and deigned to notice her. He drained the brandy glass.

"Kathryn, you look scared out of your wits. Sit down. We need to talk."

It suddenly occurred to Kat that Jules had consumed a prodigious amount from that decanter while she and the duchess had delayed in the foyer. Jules was not drunk, or even close to it, but there was a fine edge to his tone that she hadn't heard since that night in the Blue Boar Inn. Kat sat down, unsure of herself for the first time since her come-out ball.

She remained perfectly still in the chair across from where he sprawled, gazing into the fire. Her eyes studied his thick, black hair where it fell across his forehead, and the long, thin fingers that brushed it back. His eyelid was half-closed and she saw how his heavy black lashes neatly fanned his high cheekbone.

Suddenly he lifted his head and stared at her. "How did you find yourself in that antechamber with Sir Edmund?"

It was not what she had expected him to ask so she hesitated a moment too long.

"You didn't have an ... an assignation with him!" he barked out.

"Of course not! Although this is not the first time he has accosted me," she said quietly.

146

"What are you talking about, Kathryn?" Jules bellowed, lunging out of the chair, the glass and decanter forgotten on the floor beside it.

She rose to confront him. Kat had always faced her problems squarely and honestly. If she had done this in the first place perhaps Jules could have been spared the attack in Champagne.

"I am saying that since we left the boat this is my second, well, perhaps I should say, third encounter with the man."

"Would you please be so kind as to explain to me, in detail, what transpired on each of these occasions?" he asked, deadly quiet, although his gaze burned with anger.

"The first was in the garden of that French inn where we stopped for the night. He . . . he wanted me to know he would not forget my interference with Caroline. The second . . . well, the second . . ." she stumbled over the words, not quite certain how to go on.

"Yes?" he drawled, that devilish eyebrow raised.

"The second was when he sent the Contessa Primavetta to the opera box while you were in the hall," she rushed on, fearing his reaction. "And the third was tonight."

He shook his head, as if to clear it. "Kathryn, I—"

"Don't bother to explain." She shrugged with feigned indifference. "Sir Edmund made it clear you had not taken up with her again. . . . Where are you going!" she gasped, as he blurted an expletive and stalked toward the door.

"This earth has been defiled long enough by Sir Edmund's miserable existence," he spit out.

Kat threw herself in front of the library doors,

barring the way. "No! That's why I didn't tell you before! I don't want you or Jacko killed in some duel! Look at what you've already lost dueling!" Frightened tears streamed down her cheeks.

He stopped short, all the anger melting out of his face.

"My dear girl, why would you think I lost my sight in a duel?" he asked softly.

Although her face burned in embarrassment, Kat stiffened with indignation. "Since I know nothing about your past, and your thoughts and emotions you keep hidden from me, I make mistakes. I have nothing to guide me. You do not see fit to confide in me even though I am your wife."

There was a short silence, during which Kat thought her heart would break from the pain in her chest.

Then Jules smiled, a sweeter smile than she'd ever seen, and taking her hands, led her to a chair. He sat before her on a footstool. When she tried to speak, he silenced her with two fingers across her lips.

"Kathryn, I am no heroic figure. I gained my scars neither by bravery in battle or reckless daring on the dueling field." Now he hesitated for a moment, but Kat wisely did not speak. Jules gripped her hands so tightly her fingers were numb, but she did not pull away.

"I lost my sight in a family accident," he began quietly. "It's a long and tragic story." He paused for a moment. "My mother didn't love her husband, Dominic's father. They both used us as pawns in their game to hurt each other. And although I was five years older than Dominic and tried to protect him ... It didn't work ... I didn't realize until re-

148

cently how much the events had affected me." He loosened her hands at last and turned his head slightly away.

"My mother was devoted to me, unusual . . . unhealthy devotion. I was blind to the innuendo of the whole situation until it was too late. She was, after all, my mother, even if she was also an evil, spiteful woman." He turned to look Kat full in the face.

"Suffice it to say, in a drunken fit of rage my stepfather killed my mother and wounded me because he believed us to be lovers. Then he turned the gun upon himself." His voice gained strength. "Dominic also believed it for ten long years. I returned to England last year for the sole purpose of forcing him to see the truth. That the tragedy was not of our making, but of our parents. And, at last, with the help of Juliana, he has. I have regained my brother."

His words reached her, but it was a moment before understanding dawned. He was as pale as the white marble of the fireplace, but his gaze was dark with anguish.

Through the painful jolting in her ribs and the agony in her throat, Kat whispered, "I am sorry you suffered so unjustly. I wish I could take away the pain."

Kat saw his breath leave him silently and color return to flush his high cheekbones. Then with a ragged breath, he lifted her fingers to his mouth. "You have taken away the pain, Kathryn."

She couldn't speak, she couldn't even breathe, she simply rose slowly to her feet with him.

Wordlessly, he reached to caress the base of her throat with his knuckles and Kat felt the rhythm of her pulse increase under his touch. She stood utterly still, gazing up with sweet uncertainty.

Capturing her face in his hands, he moved it ever so gently from side to side, dragging her lips across his, teasing, intoxicating her. Unable to stop herself, she slid her arms around his neck and clung to him. She pressed closer to him, her mouth finally meeting his in a deep clinging kiss that left them both trembling.

He cradled her against his chest, one hand on her cheek, his lips playing over her curls. "Kathryn, we—"

"No! Promise me . . ." she faltered, throwing back her head to meet his melting gaze. "Promise me you won't place yourself in any more danger. I don't wish to lose you now . . . now that we are . . . we are becoming . . . better acquainted."

His arms tightened around her, his face was luminous with emotion. "I promise, Kathryn. And I promise that very, very soon we shall be even better acquainted."

Chapter 12

KAT STRETCHED LAZILY in her bed, then absently slid her palm over the place where Jules would be tonight if she had anything to say about it. Which, she pledged, she most definitely would!

A rush of heat spread through her body as she curled up in a tight ball thinking about him. How could one's life change so quickly? Everything was changed since she and Jules had talked. She had not realized her feelings could grow even stronger and brighter than they already were, but last night when he had told her about his accident she had been consumed with wanting to banish his pain forever and fill that hollow with love—her love.

The only blemish on an otherwise totally satisfactory evening—seeing Sir Edmund get his just deserts (when had she turned into such a blood-thirsty creature?) and discovering Jules had not renewed his liaison with the contessa—was that he had not swept Kat up in his arms in the library and carried her to his chamber.

Sighing, she moved her cheek on the pillow where his ebony head would rest tonight. She would twine her fingers through his rich locks and press kisses across that hard muscular chest. . . . Breathing most unevenly, Kat sat up in bed, her heart pounding beneath her night shift. Did all married women have these wonderful dreams about their husbands? How did one ever get anything accomplished with these delicious thoughts filling one's mind? It was quite shocking to realize she would be content to laze here all day thinking about Jules, but to make these daydreams spin true she had things to do.

Tonight, Mariah would be officially engaged to the man of her dreams. Tonight, Kat would use every lure she knew to draw Jules to her; she would entice her husband to her bed where she would entwine him forever with silken bonds of love. There was nothing standing between them and nothing, she promised herself, would stop her!

It was too early for the ton to be riding on Rotten Row, which was precisely why Jules was there. The sun's light was weak through a light layer of clouds, and there was a dawn breeze from the Thames which, thankfully, had cleansed the acrid city air. He felt wonderful this morning, free as he hadn't been in years. Somehow, in telling Kathryn about the accident, he had evacuated that hollow of pain. Now, little by little, he could share all his past with her, share all his thoughts and feelings. He never could have anticipated her reaction to his story. That was one of the reasons he hadn't wanted to burden her with it. So few people knew the truth. Now, suddenly, the past held little importance for him. The future was what mattered. His future with Kathryn.

Holding her in his arms last night, hope had sprung fresh that very soon he could keep the vow he made in Champagne. Although Kat had not actually said the words, her sweet, responsive body spoke its own language. What it had told him fueled his determination.

At Lady Tutwilliger's tonight he would charm and beguile his wife with loving attention. Perhaps this was the night that blasted connecting door would finally be opened.

Jules was jarred out of his pleasant dreams of Kathryn by a friendly crack of laughter.

"By gad, Saville, nearly ran me over!" Jacko reined his horse in sharply to sidestep Noir.

"Jacko, what a surprise! These are hardly the hours you keep. Usually you're not abroad until afternoon," Jules drawled, with a quirk of his lip.

"Making good my escape, Saville. If you're smart you'll do the same." Jacko nodded sagely. "Stay away from the house today or the women will be bound to drag you into some job for this ball of Willy's. Seen it happen before. Doesn't help I don't live at Tutwilliger House, they even find me in my rooms."

"Plan to avoid them all day, Jacko?" Jules smiled at his brother-in-law's fresh dimpled face, so much like Kathryn's.

"Got it all planned. Ride in the park this morning. Spot of lunch. Dress for the ball early, then off to faro at Mrs. Cathage's before I have to do the pretty tonight."

"Mrs. Cathage's?" Jules lifted his brow at the mention of the notorious faro den. "Bit too far on the fringe, isn't it, Jacko?"

He shrugged, moving his horse back a few paces. "Percy and Glady are going with me. Play is fair there even if the company is a bit off. Well, must be going, Saville. Remember what I told you. Stay away from Kat today, sure to put you to work."

Amusement curling his mouth, Jules watched his young brother-in-law canter down the path. Actually, he would be tied up most of the day with his man of business so he did not plan to see Kathryn. The separation only fanned the anticipation for the evening to come, Jules decided.

With a short laugh of excitement, Jules gave Noir his head, since they were quite alone, and galloped up Rotten Row.

Everything was perfection, Lady Tutwilliger decided, giving one last twist to the turban feather brushing her cheek. Dressed in her favorite color of lilac satin, Gwynneth was ready to accept the congratulations and envy of the ton. She had pulled it off: this season Kat had married the dashing and extremely well-connected Comte de Saville; now Mariah was betrothed to Mr. Christian Vanderworth—even without a title, his enormous wealth made him an enviable catch.

This Gwynneth had accomplished even in the face of the Thistlewait Jilting Scandal. Although the children's mother, Bettina, had been a sweet child, she could never have been considered a lady, and was certainly a misalliance for Francis. But, it was all ending like a fairy tale.

Gwynneth sighed, taking one last turn about the ballroom to check the floral arrangements and the fragile gilt chairs set against the walls for the dowagers. Francis and Bettina had been gloriously happy in the few years they had together and now their children had also made love matches. Although, it wasn't official by any means, it was plain

Jacko and Caroline were made for one another. That young woman had made her scamp into a very pretty-behaved man. She had even settled the slight difficulty of finding a proper match for *Miss* Vanderworth by encouraging her friendship with Gladstone Pennington. Yes, they would do nicely, also. Really, she never realized before what a genius she had for matchmaking.

Positioning herself in the entrance hall, Gwynneth had nothing to do but wait for Mariah to make her appearance. Glancing up at the hall clock, she could see Mr. Vanderworth had fifteen minutes before he was due to arrive and, as always, he would be punctual.

When the knocker pounded five minutes later she was startled out of her complicated wedding plans. Westley opened the door to admit her godson, followed by Sir Percy Allendale and Gladstone Pennington. She was totally flabbergasted. These young rips were never on time for a social engagement! It was apparent they were arguing fiercely.

"Jacko, don't be a fool! You ca—" Gladstone was heard to say before Jacko cut him off with a epithet which Gwynneth just barely made out.

"*Jacko*, what is the *meaning* of this!" she bellowed, fanning herself briskly with her lilac-tinted ostrich feathers.

All three gentlemen turned blank faces to her, although Jacko's eyes seemed overly brilliant tonight.

"We've come to celebrate my sister's engagement, Willy," Jacko smiled brightly. Too brightly, Gwynneth realized when he bent to kiss her cheek. "Where are Mariah and Caroline?" he asked, peering up the great stairway to the second floor.

"Since you are a full half hour early, they are still dressing," Gwynneth announced, pinning both Gladstone and Percy with her sharp eye. "I've known Jacko since his birth cry, so I know when he's up to something. Which one of you is going to tell me?"

Both young men looked satisfactorily terrified, but neither dared open his mouth. Jacko suddenly took her fingers, lifting them to his firm lips.

"Have I ever told you, I love you, Willy," he whispered, a heartbreaking smile filling his gorgeous face.

Stunned into speechlessness, Gwynneth stood stock still. A rustle of skirts brought all their attention to the stairs. Mariah glided down, glorious in palest pink crepe, with two glossy brown curls falling daringly down her neck. Floating behind her in a gossamer gown of azure came Caroline. Her eyes immediately lit on Jacko.

"Lord Thistlewait, you are here so early!" she breathed in unfeigned delight.

Gladstone and Percy stepped aside so Jacko could take each girl by the hand to lead them forward. "I have come early to gaze upon your beauty," Jacko drawled with unadulterated flattery.

Mariah tapped his arm playfully with her fan. "You're talking to your sister, you ninny. What really brings you?"

He pinched her cheek. "Wanted to see you, that's all. But now I must lose you to your fiancé," he laughed as the knocker sounded and Westley admitted Mr. Vanderworth. "Come, Caroline," he insisted, tucking her hand into the crook of his arm. "Let us be the first to sample the champagne Willy is serving tonight."

"What is Jacko up to?" Mariah quizzed, but Gwynneth could only shake her head. Before she could stop them, Gladstone and Percy had also disappeared up the stairs and into the ballroom. Short of racing after them, Gwynneth was powerless.

"I don't know," she said softly. "But before the evening is finished, I shall find out!"

It was fortunate that the duchess shared their carriage for Kat's nerves were so fragile she doubted she could have survived the journey alone with Jules.

All day she had been concentrating on just how she would entice her husband. She'd decided on her lowest cut gown and her hair worn the way he had admired. But by the time he handed her up into the carriage she was nearly faint from anticipation. He, on the other hand, appeared his usual dashing self, dressed in severe black and an unruffled white shirt.

Fortunately they were early enough to beat the crush of carriages. The house looked particularly festive; Willy had fashioned two floral pieces to stand on either side of the doorway. After greeting Mariah and Christian, Kat was surprised when Willy stepped out of the receiving line to pull her behind a large potted plant.

"Willy, what are you doing?" Kat questioned, concerned by the lines of worry crisscrossing her godmother's usually jovial countenance.

"Keep an eye on your twin, Kathryn. Something is up. I'm sure of it," she declared.

The tiniest black cloud appeared on Kat's rosy horizon, but she immediately banished it. "Don't worry, Willy. I'll have a talk with him," she promised, kissing her godmother's cheek.

Seemingly satisfied, Willy rejoined Mariah and Christian while Kat slipped into the ballroom to find Jules waiting for her.

"Here you are, my dear. I thought you might like a glass of champagne. Is something wrong?" he asked perceptively, in much the same voice he had used on the journey to France. The voice of strength and trust, the voice she had come to love.

"No," she smiled and glanced away to search the rapidly filling room. "Have you seen Jacko?"

"Yes, there he is, dancing with Caroline," Jules replied, touching her arm.

And there Jacko was, her twin, doing a remarkably fluid waltz with Caroline. When they glided by he threw Kat a kiss.

Laughing, Kat looked up into Jules's face and found him so close she leaned back a little upon his shoulder. "He seems fine, doesn't he?"

"He is enjoying himself. Come, let us do likewise."

He handed her glass to a passing waiter and drew her onto the floor. They fit together so perfectly. Daringly she rested her cheek against his chest, closing her eyes. She was rewarded by his arm tightening about her waist, drawing her closer than any patroness of Almack's would approve—even for a married couple.

"Kathryn, I'm keeping you all to myself tonight," he whispered into her ear, his breath fanning her skin, sending shivers down her spine.

He was a man of his word, cavalierly sending away all who sought to partner her. They danced only together. Each time they waltzed he held her

158

a bit tighter and even went so far, once, to press a kiss at the side of her neck.

Breathlessly, she pulled back to stare at him, her eyes wide with assumed shock. "Jules, what will people think?"

His arms tightened and she felt his thigh press against hers through the thin fabric of her gown.

"They will think the Comte de Saville is enchanted with his wife," Jules murmured, his gaze roaming boldly from the low-cut bodice of her gown to meet her eyes.

Weak with longing, Kat nearly missed the fanfare of Willy's formal announcement and toast to Mariah's engagement to Mr. Christian Vanderworth. Most of the guests surged forward to offer their congratulations, but Jules took this opportunity to lead her out onto a tiny balcony.

The sultry night air of the city closed around them. Jules leaned back against the brick wall. He reached out, drawing her to him, his arms tightening around her so she almost lay against him. She felt the accelerated beat of his heart beneath her breasts.

Her eyes were becoming accustomed to the darkness so very faintly she could see his face, and it was transformed by his wonderful smile.

"Kathryn, will you become my wife?"

She stared at him. "I am already your wife."

Jules's hands rose to her shoulders, then slowly, deliberately, slid down to tease the inside of her elbows, near her breasts.

"Yes, we have gone through the forms, said the right words. . . . We are legally married, but I want more," he said softly. Slowly, his hand glided up to play in the locks of hair falling about her throat. "I want more, Kathryn."

Kat was hypnotized by the pleasure his touch bore.

Carefully, he pressed a light kiss upon her lips, and Kat realized she was trembling. He whispered her name softly and, in surrender, she twined her fingers through his hair, leading him to her parted lips. Their mouths clung in a long, caressing kiss, their bodies arching together, demanding to be even closer.

She breathed her answer onto his lips. "Yes, please, Jules. I want to be your wife."

Even in this dimness she saw a flame lighten his gaze. "Then come, my darling. Tonight is ours."

He led her out of the shadows and as they stepped into the ballroom they nearly collided with Jacko and Caroline. They were hidden by a drapery in the window embrasure and, to Kat's bemused shock, were clasped in a passionate embrace.

At that moment, Jacko released Caroline and, stepping back, he met Kat's eyes. What she saw on his face froze her blood. Without a word, he stalked away into the lights and music of the ball.

"Oh, Kathryn, he kissed me," Caroline whispered, touching her lips with trembling fingers. "He's never done it before. It was quite wonderful."

Kat's eyes lifted from Caroline's enraptured countenance to Jules's face.

"Kathryn, what is it?" he asked quickly.

Shaking her head, Kat was already moving across the floor. "See Caroline back into the ballroom. I must find Jacko!"

Where was he? Frantic, Kat scanned the gathering for his blond head, but couldn't find him anywhere. She caught Sir Percy skulking around in the hallway.

"Have you seen Jacko?" she demanded.

"No . . . no," he stammered, stepping back a pace. "Looking for your husband, myself."

"He's just returning to the ballroom," she replied quickly, dismissing him to survey the foyer. No Jacko. Perhaps he had gone to his old room to be alone. There was definitely something wrong; something in his eyes that Kat didn't understand, but that struck her cold with fear. Willy had been right. She shouldn't have so readily discounted her godmother's fears, but she had been preoccupied with Jules.

Even in the upper hallway the merrymaking from the ball could be plainly heard. Only as she neared Jacko's room did it fade. She pushed open the door and gasped.

With his back to her, a man stood before the oak cabinet beside the bed. It was not her twin.

"Glady, what are you doing?" she asked, shutting the door loudly.

Startled, he dropped the box he held upon the bed. Quickly, he grabbed it up and thrust it behind his back, but not before Kat had seen what it was.

"Kat, what are you doing here?" he croaked, his eyes shifting about, looking for escape.

"Why have you got Jacko's dueling pistols? And where is he?" she demanded, rushing to wrest the box away. "What is going on? You will not leave this room without telling me."

"Jacko left the ball so you couldn't find him," Glady admitted, stepping toward her. "You must give me the pistols! With his own pistols Jacko might have a chance," he continued, half under his breath.

"A chance?" she breathed, before sinking onto the bed, understanding making her knees give way. "A duel. With whom?"

"Trigge!" Glady growled, whisking the box from her suddenly numb fingers. "I've said too much. Stay out of it, Kat. And pray," he stated firmly, making his escape out the door.

Like a child, Kat had thought all her problems gone forever in the face of her love for Jules. Now all that happiness vanished to be replaced with deadly terror for Jacko.

"Whatever am I going to do?" She moaned, burying her face in her hands.

"We are going to stop him, of course."

Kat sprang to her feet, blinking several times, hardly believing her eyes. Hannah rose from a chair that had been turned to face the fireplace.

"Hannah, you heard!" Kat cried.

"Yes, dear. I came here to read and escape the noise from below. I must have dozed off and didn't awaken until you slammed the door. Then I thought it best to remain silent."

Kat was trembling, and Hannah drew her close in a gentle, lavender-scented embrace.

"What are we going to do, Hannah?" Kat whispered.

Pushing Kat to arm's length, Hannah's usually placid face was stern. "Your brother cannot be allowed to duel. You are the only person he ever listens to, so you must talk to him. If you cannot reason with him you must give him this." Reaching in her deep skirt pocket, she pulled out a small bottle of laudanum.

162

"Drug him?" Kat gasped.

Hannah shrugged. "Just enough so he misses the duel at dawn. Isn't that when these wretched men do their foolishness?"

"Yes, but if he does not appear, Trigge will just seek him out again," Kat said slowly, "or try to besmirch his honor." A seed of a terrifying idea was taking root in her appalled brain. She would never endanger Jules by asking for his help in this, for she would take care of Trigge herself.

"It buys us time," Hannah stated matter-of-factly. "Trigge is such a beast someone else might very likely do away with him before he can harm Jacko!"

Jules glanced into Lady Tutwilliger's library and, finding it empty, motioned an agitated Sir Percy in, closing the door firmly behind them. The young man had been uncharacteristically persistent to have a word alone.

"Well, what is it, Allendale?" Jules drawled, leaning one shoulder against the mantelpiece. He really had more important things on his mind this evening.

"It is Jacko," he stated baldly.

"Jacko!" Jules straightened, remembering Kat's frightened face as she went after him. "What has he gotten himself into?"

"Know you think me a sad rattle, Saville. True, of course." Sir Percy shrugged, shaking his head. "Can't seem to stop myself. Been like this since I was in short pants. But Jacko's my friend in spite of everything. He would kill me if he knew I was talking to you. But no where else to turn."

"Allendale, tell me! At once!" Jules commanded.

Nodding, Sir Percy took a deep breath. "We were playing faro at Mrs. Cathage's when Trigge came in. He had been drinking. Maybe even brawling somewhere. He's sporting a black eye and a cut lip. Soon as he sets sight on Jacko he joins our table and starts taunting him. Glady and I tried to drag Jacko away, but you know how stubborn he can be."

"Yes, yes, I know. Just tell me what occurred," Jules urged, impatient with Sir Percy's lengthy explanation.

"Said he wouldn't be driven off by that bounder!"

"Percy, cut line!"

"The short of it, Saville, is Trigge insulted Kat and Miss Strange. Jacko landed him a facer, and Trigge called him out."

"When and where is it to be?" Jules asked with cold rage.

"Dawn tomorrow. The road to Scotland. The clearing just beyond the Four Feathers Inn."

"I know the place." Jules caught Sir Percy's heart-sick look and gave him a brief smile. "You have done the right thing. Never fear, Trigge will not be meeting Jacko in the morning. I shall take care of him myself."

"Understand, Saville." Sir Percy nodded, relief flooding his face. "Knew Jacko could count on you. Now I'm going to my rooms and lock myself in for fear my damn tongue will get everyone even deeper in the suds."

"Excellent idea, Allendale." Jules stood in the foyer as Sir Percy beat a hasty retreat out the door. He himself must not be far behind. Knowing Trigge, it might take all night to unearth the bounder. But he would find him and rid the world once and for all of that canaille. Trigge would not survive until dawn to harm Jacko.

Jules turned to see Kat walking slowly down the stairs. She looked pale and frightened. At all costs he must keep this from her.

"My dear, you look tired. Come, sit in the library." He led her back into the quiet room, again closing the door.

Helping her to a chair, he knelt before her, taking her cool hands between his palms.

"Kathryn, I must leave you for a few hours," he said gently and saw her dull eyes widen.

"Why?" she whispered, and Jules could see she was having difficulty focusing her thoughts.

"I have something I must do. I will arrange for someone to see you and *Grandmère* home."

"If you don't mind, Jules, I shall stay here tonight. I . . . I was just upstairs with Hannah. She . . . she isn't well. I would like to stay with her tonight."

Icy dread stilled his hands where they slowly massaged her fingers. "This has nothing to do with your looking for Jacko, does it?" he asked carefully.

"I couldn't find him." She smiled weakly. "If you see him would you tell him I demand he attend me."

"Of course. Now I must be off." Rising, he pulled her slowly to her feet. He stroked her cheek with his fingertip. "I regret this interruption to our evening. Tonight, after all, shall not be ours." He pressed a gentle kiss on her cool lips before starting toward the door.

"Jules!"

At her anguished cry he swung around and she ran into his embrace, throwing her arms around

165

his neck. Startled, Jules pulled her tightly to him as she lifted her face.

"Kiss me," she whispered.

Responding to her urgency, Jules crushed her to him. Her lips parted, drawing him into her sweetness.

At last, Jules slowly pulled away, gazing with longing into Kat's upturned face, her aquamarine eyes wide with commitment.

"Tomorrow shall be ours, Jules, I promise."

Chapter 13

Hᴀɴɴᴀʜ ʜᴇʟᴘᴇᴅ Kᴀᴛ sneak out the servant's entrance. A hired hack was waiting, also by Hannah's design, and Kat slipped into it, keeping the hood of her old black cloak tightly about her face. If she hadn't been so worried about her brother she might have wondered at Hannah's adept handling of the whole situation.

Within a very few minutes she was let down at Jacko's rooms. She peered around, very much as if she were a housebreaker, but this was a mission of the utmost delicacy. Her knocks echoed into the quiet corridor, again making her look nervously about. It would not do to raise an alarm or to wake Jacko's valet. She knocked again, a bit louder. Surely her twin was here, preparing himself for the duel. Dawn was not that far away she realized, fresh fear making her pound harder.

"By gad, what—" Jacko bellowed and opened the door. She pushed her way in. "Kat! What the devil are you doing here?"

He had been lying down, she could see that by his mussed curls and flushed face, but he was fully dressed in buckskins and a lawn shirt, open at the throat.

Dropping her cloak over a chair, she turned to

167

him. "I have come to talk some sense into you!"
Their identical eyes met in complete understanding
and, slowly, he shut the door, leaning against it.

"Which one of my *friends* was fool enough to tell
you?" he questioned, cold anger paling his cheeks.

"No one *told* me, Jacko. I discovered Glady
sneaking out of your room with the dueling pistols.
I doubt they are for target practice!" She folded her
arms across her breasts as she glared at him. "It
doesn't matter, anyway. Because I am not allowing
you to duel!"

Pushing away from the door, he strolled past her
to a small table that held a decanter and glasses.
He poured a glass of brandy and quickly tipped it
down his throat. "I am past the age where you can
lead me around on a string, Kat," he said wearily,
turning to her. "I know you think you must be my
keeper. Cover up my pranks and mind my scraped
knees when I fall. But you cannot fix this, twin.
This is something for me alone."

The very fact that he was deadly quiet and un-
characteristically serious coiled fingers of terror
through every fiber of her body. No mere words of
hers would dissuade him this time. She had no
choice but to carry out the daring plan that had
been flourishing in her mind since talking with
Hannah. She refused to think about the possible
consequences. It was the only way she could save
her brother.

"I see," she said quietly, dropping down upon the
edge of his mussed bed. "Can I at least stay until
Glady comes for you?"

"I'm meeting him there." A ghost of a smile
twitched his firm mouth. "Refuse to listen to him

168

ring a peal over me all the way to the Scotland Road."

"Scotland! The duel is in Scotland?" she exclaimed, momentarily at a loss. She didn't even know how to get to Scotland.

"Of course it isn't in Scotland!" he scoffed in a more normal tone. "The Four Feathers is only . . . no, you don't, Kat! I'm not telling you where the duel will take place!"

"Of course you're not," she soothed, patting the bed beside her. "Come sit beside me so I can weep all over your chest."

With a rueful smile he sat down, sliding his arm around her shoulders. "Glad you're not having hysterics or being a watering pot," he murmured, resting his cheek on her hair. "Couldn't take that on top of everything else."

"Which is precisely why I am using such restraint. I've always understood you, haven't I, Jacko?"

"Always," he grinned, pinching her cheek. "That's why I stayed away from you at the ball, Kat. Knew you'd sense something was up."

"Yes, well, now I must just help you get ready for this." She sprang to her feet, taking his glass from where it dangled in his fingers. "Let me pour you another brandy, Jacko. And if you don't mind, I'll have one myself."

"A brandy for you? Saville teach you the pleasure of a good tipple, Kat?" Jacko essayed a smile.

"Yes, Jules has taught me much. . . . Did you hear something in the hall, Jacko? I hope Jules has not followed me here," she feigned alarm.

Her twin went to the door to peer out into the

169

hall. In that moment Kat poured the entire vial of laudanum into his brandy.

"No one there," he said, turning back to take the glass from her fingers and sit down again beside her.

Kat held her breath, taking one small sip of brandy. It burned all the way down. How could men tip it down their throats so easily as Jacko was doing?

"Will you promise me to remember everything I've told you about firing," Kat asked, carefully watching his flushed face.

"I've thought of nothing else all night," he admitted ruefully, taking another deep drink, draining the glass. "I'm not really that bad a shot, am I, Kat?"

"Well, I . . ." she began in a slightly lower tone, but stopped when he yawned, blinking his eyes.

"What was I saying?" he inquired, a funny little frown on his face. "Mind wandering. Thinking about our target practice in France. Caroline saying it didn't matter . . ."

"What about Caroline?" Kat dropped her voice to a whisper, her heart thumping as his lids began to droop over his eyes.

"Funny about Caroline . . . somehow always thinking about the minx . . ." Shaking his head, he shut his eyes, taking a deep breath. "Don't know what . . ."

Forcing his lids open, he stared at her and she saw understanding radically alter his face into a hard incredulous mask. "Kat . . . what have . . . ?" Unable to keep himself upright, Jacko suddenly crumpled to the bed behind him.

Kat bit hard on her lower lip to stop it trembling

as hot aching tears burned her eyes. Brushing his curls back, she pressed a kiss on his forehead. "I'm sorry, Jacko, but I couldn't let you be killed. At least I will have a chance," she whispered.

Drying her tears with an edge of the coverlet, she scrambled to her feet and began to unbutton her dress. She must hurry. The Scotland Road was on the other side of the city and she had no idea how far north the Four Feathers was located, but somehow she would find it.

Twenty minutes later, Kat stood in front of the mirror, twisting every which way. Jacko's buckskins were tight, but they would do. She slipped a vest over the lawn shirt before pulling on his coat. She'd have to keep the vest on during the duel to conceal the swell of her breasts. She had to pull this deception off. No one could ever know.

There was only one last thing that must be done. She pulled the pins from her hair and it fell heavily about her shoulders.

She hoped Jules would not mind, too much, having a wife who resembled a boy. Oh Jules! Would they ever have their night of love that he had so sweetly promised?

Steadfastly, she pushed all thoughts of Jules away. If he knew about the duel he might challenge Trigge himself. There was a nagging worry of doubt in the back of her mind that his sudden and urgent business might have something to do with this duel. But how could he know?

She mustn't think about that now. She must concentrate on protecting Jacko and Jules, by getting rid of Sir Edmund. Jacko was sure to be killed in any confrontation with that monster, and Jules's blind eye would surely hamper him in a duel. She

171

couldn't take any chance that harm might come to either one of them. She loved her twin as if he were an extension of herself. But her feelings for Jules were entirely different—that love was so newly discovered, so precious, she could hardly bear to think of it, to think of all she was risking. With a sinking heart, she only hoped he would be able to understand.

Taking a bunch of her hair, she lifted the scissors, closed her eyes and snipped. In a surprisingly short time blond curls covered the floor at her feet. Running her fingers through what was left of her hair, she fluffed it around her face. This was the best she could do. Snatching up Jacko's hat she rammed it on her head and looked.

Her brother's countenance stared back at her from the mirror.

Quickly she let herself out before she could change her mind. She must hurry if she was to find the Four Feathers in time.

The clock was ticking down and Jules had not unearthed Trigge. He had prowled through every faro house, gaming hell, and bagnio he could think of, but no Trigge. Discreet questioning had added not a clue. Mrs. Cathage had been ingratiating, but no assistance; after challenging Jacko, she said Trigge had simply disappeared.

But he would have to surface in the field beyond the Four Feathers at dawn to meet Jacko. However, unbeknownst to Trigge there would be a change of plans. Jules would face him at dawn, not Kat's impetuous twin.

He must protect Kat from all this. If she knew Jacko was in danger she would be sick with worry.

She need never know, he consoled himself. He would dispatch Trigge in a few hours. He couldn't conceive there would be one cry of protest to the crown; this earth would be better off without the blighter.

Then he would return to Kat and sweep her off for their night of love. It didn't matter if their night began before breakfast. Funny, even through his outrage he ached for her.

Jacko refused to answer Jules's knocks that steadily escalated into noisy banging. He couldn't be gone already, Jules hoped. He took two steps back, preparing to break down the damn door when Jacko's valet appeared at the end of the hall.

Holding a candle before him, he hurried forward. "Monsieur le Comte, is something wrong?"

"Yes! Open Lord Thistlewait's door. I must see him on urgent family business," Jules commanded and was immediately obeyed. The room was lit by a single guttering candle, showing Jacko sprawled across the bed.

"Leave us!" Jules ordered and the door was immediately closed.

"Good god, Jacko, how can you sleep at a time like this!" Jules stormed, stalking to the bed. He bent to shake his shoulder. The moment he saw how deeply Jacko slept he knew something was very wrong.

He glanced around the room. The cloak and dress neatly draped over the chair stopped his heart, his blood running cold through every fiber of his body. Surely not! Kat wouldn't—

Taking a long breath into his strained lungs, he walked forward, touched the gown, and forced him-

173

self to accept the outrageous idea that had struck him. Kat's perfume still clung to the fabric.

"No," he growled, shaking his head, rejecting his thoughts. Then he saw her beautiful long hair littering the floor in front of the mirror. That discovery drove all doubt away. Kat would!

Once he had believed no pain could ever be greater than the night his mother, in her drunkenness, mistook him for his late father and drove Charles Crawford to murder and suicide. That night he had lost his eye. The aftermath had shattered his life, Dominic's world. It had taken more than ten years to heal those wounds. But, finally, the brothers had come to understand and accept that they bore no blame.

That pain was as nothing to the icy fear that washed over him, drowning him in terror for Kat. She was taking her twin's place on the dueling field. His Kat would be facing a murderer and a cheat across forty paces of mist-shrouded earth.

"No!" he raged, striding to the door to fling it open. Jacko's valet hovered nervously in the hallway.

"Wake Lord Thistlewait as soon as you can. Tell him all is well, but he must get to Culter House as soon as possible," Jules ordered.

Fortunately Noir was fresh and eager, as always, for a gallop. The horse surged forward under Jules's heels, clattering loudly through the sleeping London streets. The Four Feathers was well north on the Scotland Road, Jules knew, and, already, the sky was more gray than black.

Icy terror drove him forward, numbing his mind and his heart. He had only just found true contentment—love and joy with Kat. If anything happened to her, his life would, again, be meaningless.

The postboy at the second inn she stopped at knew the Four Feathers and gave her directions. Kat arrived in the yard just as the sun was sending its first feeble rays through the early morning mist.

Sliding off Jacko's horse, she threw the reins to a postboy, and gazed around. Surely a duel couldn't be conducted in the Four Feathers stableyard?

Movement in the field north of the inn drew her attention. Slowly striding forward, taking exaggerated steps, trying to walk as much like Jacko as possible—although it was difficult in his Hessians even stuffed with stockings—she saw two groups waiting. No one paid her any notice.

Trigge was standing with a man she didn't recognize. His second, obviously not a gentleman.

Nearby, Glady talked with an older man who carried a black bag. A physician, Kat realized. The enormity of her situation, which she had ruthlessly banished, seeped back into her mind. Her insides were churning. Fear might mean discovery. Besides she couldn't disgrace her twin. She thrust up her chin. She must remain calm and aim as if at a target. Although she had no intention of killing Trigge, she did mean to aim at his shooting hand so it would be a long time, if ever, before he could issue another challenge.

Spying her, Glady rushed forward. Quickly, she turned her head as if surveying the field.

"Jacko, we've been waiting for you. Are you all right?"

Glancing out of the corner of her eye, Kat could

see Glady looked terrible. His eyes were bloodshot and his face haggard.

"You look like the devil," Kat mumbled gruffly and moved away.

"I know," Glady gasped, keeping up with her. "Got drunk as a skunk worrying about you. My valet pulled me together and put me on a horse. Still a bit blurry-eyed, Jacko." Suddenly, he grabbed Kat's arm, but she pulled away as unobtrusively as possible.

"Jacko, don't do this, old boy!" Glady pleaded, desperation filling his young face. "Give the word and I'll stop it somehow."

Tempted almost beyond reason, Kat paused and looked over at Sir Edmund Trigge. He appeared coolly comfortable. He had already shed his coat and stood waiting in his lawn shirt. His face sported a smug smile.

This man had promised to get even with her and Jacko and Jules. She knew his threats were not idle. This might be her only chance to keep them all from further harm. She shook her head in a final denial and moved to her spot, slipping out of her coat.

"Here is your pistol. Me and Trigge's second have already checked them," Glady said dully. "I'm to count off the paces. But be careful Jacko, I don't trust the man. If he tries to take advantage I'll yell—and you, dammit, will drop to the ground to protect yourself."

Kat nodded absently as she weighed the pistol in her hand, checking its balance. These were the pistols she and Jacko had learned to shoot with. An odd pastime for a girl, perhaps, but as children the Thistlewait offspring had had to find their own diversions. They had been shunned by their peers until Willy sailed into their lives, informing their father she would take them all in hand. And she had! Dearest Willy. If Kat survived this she would tell Willy how much she loved her, how well she had stood as mother to them all.

Kat stepped forward, but Glady stopped her. "What are you doing, Jacko? Remove that vest at once and the hat. They'll give him too much of a target."

The vest must stay to prevent her exposure, but Kat slowly removed the hat.

Although Glady wrinkled his brow, studying her, he didn't seem to recognize her. She knew he would never, in his wildest dreams, think Kat would take Jacko's place. For an instant, she could hardly believe it herself.

Trigge waited for her, joking with his second. Obviously he had been through this many times before. She had no choice. Slowly, she came face-to-face with him, taking one long look at his malevolence.

They stood back-to-back, their pistols raised over their right shoulders.

"Gentlemen, at my signal you shall take twenty paces forward and then turn and fire," Glady stated flatly.

Blood roared in Kat's ears, but she strained, concentrating on his words. She and Jacko had played at this as children. Jacko . . . no matter what happens you're safe. . . . The hilt of the pistol slid a little in her damp palm, but she only wrapped her fingers more tightly around it. She had so much to live for. Jules—I love you.

177

She wouldn't allow anything to defeat her. Certainly not a bounder like Sir Edmund Trigge.

"Now!" Trigge's second barked.

Glady began. "One . . ."

Kat stepped forward, her mind empty of everything except his voice.

"Two . . ."

The Four Feathers finally loomed into view but Jules galloped right past it to the north field. Silhouetted against the trees he saw the drama being played out.

"Oh, God, no," he breathed, close enough now to realize the duel was beginning.

"Please, Kat, please . . ." he prayed. Digging his heels into a winded Noir he raced forward. He had to stop them! He was close enough now to shout!

But his desperate cry was drowned out by a crack. Only one shot had been fired!

Chapter 14

THE SOUND REVERBERATED in Jules's mind . . . shot
. . . Kat . . . shot . . . Kat . . . He flung himself off
Noir and ran across to where one duelist had crumpled to the ground. In the half light he could not
distinguish who it was.

"Please, no . . ." he breathed, his chest aching as
if it were he who had been shot.

Three men hovered over the injured party.

"Saville, what are you doing here?" Glady
gasped, before Jules shoved him aside. He fell to
his knees beside the doctor.

It was Trigge.

Of a sudden he could breathe again. His head
swiveled to where Kat stood; unbelievably she was
all right. He didn't dare go to her, he would give
the whole game away. Instead he concentrated on
the villain before him.

Trigge's eyes were closed, his face devoid of all
color and his right hand hung helplessly, bleeding
profusely.

"Didn't know Jacko had it in him," Glady suddenly muttered from behind Jules's shoulder.

Slowly, Jules rose to his feet. Stepping away, he
turned and looked across the forty paces.

Still Kat had not moved; she stood, the pistol

smoking in her hand as morning mist swirled around her.

Even from this distance he could see her start of recognition when she saw him. She took one tentative step toward him.

"Stay there! I'll handle this!" he commanded harshly. His tone caused her to draw back sharply and turn away.

God, didn't she understand! He wanted nothing more than to go to her, gather her in his arms and never let her go!

His relief that she was alive was boundless, unlike anything he'd ever known. But he must keep up the pretence that she was Jacko before these men. Soon, very soon, he would show her in every way just what she meant to him. But first, he must deal with Trigge.

Swinging back, he saw Sir Edmund was now sitting up with the help of his second. Some color had returned to his face.

"He'll live," the doctor nodded, wrapping his hand with strips of gauze.

"But only for a few more minutes," Jules said calmly.

His words brought four pairs of eyes up to stare at him. Slowly, Jules peeled off one riding glove and, leaning over, slapped Sir Edmund's pale cheek.

"Sir, what are you doing!" Trigge's second sputtered.

"Prepare Sir Edmund's pistol! We duel now!" he ordered.

Jules saw fear slowly enter Trigge's suddenly alert eyes.

"You're mad, Saville! My right hand is ruined," Trigge moaned. "I can't fight you."

"It has always seemed your fondest wish to get me on the dueling field," Jules said pleasantly. "Now you have succeeded." He flicked a look to the second. "I repeat, load the pistols!"

"Sir, I must protest," the doctor interjected, rising to face Jules. "This man is in no condition to duel. That hand may never mend properly. It would be tantamount to murder."

"It is tantamount to ridding the world of vermin!" Kneeling, Jules stared into Trigge's bloodless countenance. "I warned you. Now it is too late. How does it feel to know you face your doom, Trigge? This is what your helpless victims endured." Rising, he glared down at the man who would have taken Kat's life without a thought. That brought fresh rage. "You have two minutes, then I shoot you where you lie!" Jules bit out, his fists clenched at his sides.

"No, no, wait, Saville," Sir Edmund pleaded, struggling to his feet. "I'll leave England. Go to the Continent. You'll never see me again. I give my word."

"Your word means nothing!" Jules laughed harshly. "You have one minute, Trigge."

His pallid eyes searched wildly around. "My God, someone do something! You can't let him just shoot me in cold blood!"

"Saville, old boy, just not done you know," Glady offered quietly. "Not worth it to be sent into exile. Let him go. I'll see him to the coast and make sure he boards a ship."

"I, too, shall accompany them," the doctor informed him. "My patient shall require my attention until then."

Jules stood for a long time considering. His desire for Kat, greater than that for revenge, won out.

"Your miserable life is spared, Trigge!" Jules growled, stepping away. "But get him out of my sight quickly before I change my mind!"

Sir Edmund's second obviously took Jules at his word for he very nearly dragged him across the field, the doctor following hastily.

"Right decision, old boy," Glady nodded. "I'll see the bounder off."

"Thank you, Pennington. I don't see Jacko's horse. Before you leave have the postboy bring it here from the inn. I must get him back to London."

"Jacko!" Glady glanced over to where Kat stood. "Must bid him farewell. What a shot, Saville! Proud of him!" Glady beamed.

"Take care of Trigge for us. I'll see to Jacko," Jules commanded and with a small salute Glady followed the others.

At last they were alone. He turned to Kat. She had drawn Jacko's coat on and placed his hat over her riotous curls.

Jules began to walk toward her, then he started to run. He was nearly there, was even reaching out to draw her into his arms, when the postboy ran up, holding Jacko's horse by the reins.

Kat's eyes were enormous pools of aquamarine; her cheeks were drained of all color.

"Yes, I know, it is you." Jules murmured. "Mount. We must return to London as quickly as possible."

Kat took the reins and flung herself into the saddle. Jules flipped a guinea to the astonished postboy. Wheeling Noir, he led her from the field of honor, gathering speed as they passed the Four

182

Feathers. They were miles south before Jules slowed to a trot, Kat beside him.

Nervously, she slid him a frightened look. "Jules, please let me explain. . . ."

"Incroyable!" Jules lapsed into French in astonishment. "You are unbelievable! Here I ride *ventre à terre* to save you, and you, my beautiful wife, have saved the day." His dark eyes turned stern. "Never do anything like this again. You must promise me!"

"I promise," Kat returned firmly. "I hope never to be so frightened again. But, Jules," she put her hand on his arm to stop the horses. "I did it!" Her voice was full of pride and wonder.

"Yes, but now we have no time to waste, Kat. We must have you safely back in town and inform Jacko of his exploit on the field of honor today or all might be lost."

He was holding himself tightly in check. There was nothing he wished for but to be able to take her in his arms and tell her how proud he was of her, that the courage she possessed amazed him, that he loved her. But he couldn't do that, here, on the open highway. So he urged her forward.

They were in luck; the city traffic was still thin so they were able to weave their way through it quickly to Culter House.

They slid off their horses and stood facing one another in the mews. Excitement warred with apprehension, marring the beauty of Kat's eyes. Her delectable lips quivered slightly.

Unable to contain himself, Jules stepped closer. "My beautiful wife," he murmured, steeling every fiber of his body not to touch her just yet. "I'm not angry with you. On the contrary, the moment we get inside and I have you to myself, I am going to

183

remove every article of Jacko's clothing and kiss each sweet silken inch of your body."

Jules smiled in delight as Kat's cheeks flushed a brilliant scarlet. He saw, with joy, the response in her eyes.

"My lord," Kat breathed, suddenly finding it difficult to take air into her lungs. "I think we should enter immediately."

With a joyful laugh, Jules clasped her arm, leading her up the short flight of steps.

They had not reached the door before it was flung open. There in the wide rectangle back hallway stood Kat's entire family, except for Jacko, and the Duchess of Culter.

"You're all here!" Kat gasped, meeting Willy's shrewd eyes.

"Kathryn!" Willy shrieked, her hand clasped to her throat. *"I need my smelling salts!"*

"I think she means it this time!" Kat cried, rushing forward as Lady Tutwilliger crumpled into the arms of one of the Culter footmen.

With Jules's help they carried her up to the main salon and laid her gently upon the blue velvet couch. Carefully, Mariah arranged pillows under her head while Kat burned a feather beneath her nose.

"Kathryn, I didn't expect you to change places with Jacko!" Hannah scolded, wringing her hands over Lady Tutwilliger. "When I told Gwynneth this morning about our plan, she flew up into the boughs. We rushed over here to stop you but were too late."

"You're not hurt! Did you kill him, Kat?" Mariah asked softly, her Thistlewait eyes glistening with revenge. "The bounder deserves to die!"

184

"No, he lives. I hit his pistol hand before he got a shot away," Kat said carefully, trembling ever so slightly, remembering Glady's precise count ... twirling at twenty paces, and firing at Sir Edmund's hand as if it were nothing more than a target.

Lady Tutwilliger, under their combined ministrations, began to stir, her lashes fluttering wildly before she opened her lids.

"Willy, dearest, I'm sorry for frightening you," Kat soothed, kissing her cheek. "Everything's all right now."

"But, where is Jacko?" she demanded, recovering to pin Kat with a steely stare.

"Oh, yes, where is Jacko! He could have been killed!" Caroline cried, leaping from the deep wing chair where she had collapsed in a bout of tears.

"I'm here," a weary voice called from the doorway. Her twin stood, leaning heavily against the wood, his lawn shirt open at the throat below a face ashen with fear. "Kat?"

She ran to him, and he gathered her fiercely close so she could feel how fast his heart was beating. "Please forgive me, Jacko. I didn't know what else to do," she sobbed into his chest, relief that she had saved him finally cracking the dam of desperation she had somehow kept in check.

Her head jerked back as he gripped her shoulders, and shook her. "Forgive you! I should give you the thrashing of your life for being so foolhardy!"

"Oh, you beast!" Caroline cried, flying forward to pummel his arm with her small fists. He let go of his sister to protect himself.

"Caroline, what in—?"

"Oh, be quiet, you brute!" she sobbed. "If Kat hadn't been so brave and daring you would be lying on that dueling field. And if you died my life would be over!"

Sobbing, she threw herself against his chest, and Jacko wasted no time in taking the opportunity to kiss her.

Kat felt Jules come up behind her and she leaned back into his embrace.

"I know exactly how she feels," Jules murmured seductively into her ear, causing a strange ache low in her abdomen.

"Well, that settles that!" Lady Tutwilliger declared, making a remarkable recovery. She rose from the couch to flick out the folds of her gown. "I assume you have enough places set for breakfast, Sybilla."

The duchess lifted her chin, sniffing. "I am always prepared for guests, Gwynneth."

"Kathryn and I will not be joining you," Jules drawled, pulling his unresisting wife toward the doorway. "We are retiring."

As he dragged her out of the salon, Kat heard a little murmur of pleased shock from her family before they began to discuss Jacko's imminent engagement to Caroline.

"Jules, I . . . what are you doing!"

To the obvious horror of two footmen, Jules swept her up in his arms. The Hessian on her left foot fell off.

He lifted that wonderful eyebrow in question and she shrugged. "They are much too large for me. Jacko will find it."

At the top of the stairs she wiggled her foot and

the other boot was discarded to tumble down the steps.

Jules glanced at it and Kat smiled, nestling against his chest. "I am simply helping you."

She felt his laughter, and turning her face, pressed a kiss on his neck. A pulse leapt to life beneath her lips.

Jules kicked her bedroom door shut behind them and placed her carefully, barefoot, on the floor.

Then he kept his unspoken promise—boldly unlocking the door between their chambers. "This door shall remain open always." It was a command she would be happy to comply with.

She turned to go into her dressing room to find her prettiest night robe, the one from their wedding.

"Where are you off to, wife?" he demanded. "I'm never letting you out of my sight again!"

Once more, he swung her up in his arms, and in two strides they fell onto the bed together.

An instant later, somehow, he had removed his coat and hers.

"Jules, how . . . ?" Her words were smothered by a deep kiss, his lips teasing hers open so she could draw him even closer to her.

Bemused, she lay in his arms as he began to undress her. With each shirt button undone, he pressed a searching kiss on her heated skin. "I've been wanting to do this since our wedding night when I realized I loved you," he murmured, his skillful fingers moving to the trouser buttons.

"Why didn't you?" she asked, cupping his cheeks to draw his face to hers. As he had done to her, she dragged his lips across her mouth. "Why didn't you?"

187

"I wanted to woo you . . . make you love me." He searched her eyes, a tiny shadow of doubt in his chocolate gaze. She must eradicate it at once!

More deftly than she believed her trembling fingers could be, she began to unbutton his shirt. "I vowed I would only marry for love. I kept that promise."

"Kathryn, I love you," he whispered, his searching lips brushing the shoulder her shirt slid from.

"Jules," she breathed against the hard tawny chest she had spied the first instant she laid eyes upon him. "This is exactly how we met. On a bed, both in scandalous states of undress. Did you ever dream it would turn out like this?"

Sliding his fingers into her curls, gently, he tilted her head back so their gaze entwined.

"My darling, it was our destiny."